D1384928

Come Aboard
And
Bring your
Dory!

ELISABETH OGILVIE

Come Aboard And Bring your Dory!

McGRAW-HILL BOOK COMPANY

New York · Toronto · London · Sydney

HOUSTON PUBLIC LIBRARY

We are grateful to the publishers, James S. Kerr, 79 Berkeley Street, Glasgow, C.3, for permission to reproduce the song appearing on pages 141 and 176.

Library of Congress Catalog Card Number: 69-16258

1234567890 VBVB 754321069

T HE DUSK was coming in like the tide and filling Cameron Cove by the time Geordie had set his bait aboard for the next day's hauling and put the boat back on her mooring. Rowing ashore stern first and pushing on the oars, he could see the evening star shining big and white in the clear blue-green western sky over the black sawtooth line of spruces. The house windows were yellow rectangles against the velvet shadow of the woods. Otherwise no one could tell at this moment that a house was there.

As Geordie walked up the path toward the lights, the weight of sadness that had oppressed him for the past week was lifted somewhat by the knowledge that the family would be alone tonight. The last of his mother's relatives had left this morning, saying with a significant glance at the twins' red heads, "I'll be expecting to hear from you pretty soon."

Don't hold your breath, Geordie had felt like telling him. Now he shook off the man as if he were one of the late mosquitoes humming around, and swung his rubber boots faster toward the house. In the entry he smelled the sharp fragrance of apples heaped in baskets all around him as he kicked off his boots. Last year at apple time he'd come home at night with his father, and his mother had been in the kitchen.

This year—within two months of each other—both were gone, Marm only a week ago.

He rubbed his big hands hard over his face as if to wipe away what must be there, then walked into the heat and noise and light. Geordie Cameron, twenty years old, six feet three in his socks, lean and big nosed, his jaw lean and strong. His coarse, coal-glinting black hair wouldn't lie back; he had peaked black eyebrows, and under them his eyes were a light, intense, and stinging blue.

Lucy, trying to get Penn away from the telephone and the twins off the floor, was so relieved to see her older brother that she felt like crying. She wasn't ordinarily a tearful sort, but this had been a hideous week. However, one look at Geordie's face and she blinked back her own misery.

"Genie, you put the beans on the table," she said briskly to the fourteen-year-old girl. "Geordie, can you do anything about those boys?"

Harold the dog bounded joyfully at Geordie, who scratched behind the big mongrel shepherd's ears and said, "Why, this is a pretty good boy, I'd say."

"That boy's the best of the bunch," said Lucy.

The ten-year-old twins crashed into Geordie's legs. He bent down and took a twin in each big hand, hauled them up and stood them on their feet. Panting, they glared at him.

"You fellers get your faces and hands washed, and your hair combed," said Geordie. *"Right now."* He shoved them toward the sink, then turned toward the far corner of the big kitchen where Penn sat on a tall stool, leaning against the wall and talking intimately into the telephone.

"Supper's ready, Penn," Geordie called. "Bid her farewell or I'll do it for you." He took a long step toward the corner and Penn said hastily, "See you," and hung up. His strong cheekbones were blazing red. He was almost as tall as Geordie and had the same coloring, but where Geordie looked rugged, Penn was handsome. "I pay my share of that telephone!"

"That's got nothing to do with it. Your sisters have a meal on the table. And while we're about it, from now on when Lucy speaks to you, you pay attention, and you answer." He turned to the twins and pointed a finger at them. "And *you* mind Lucy and Genie both. That clear?" Harold stared with glowing amber eyes at Geordie's finger and barked.

Geordie shook the finger at him. "And *you* behave yourself, too." The twins burst out laughing, and scrambled hungrily into their chairs.

Penn slid silently into his place. Lucy gave him a little pat on the shoulder as she set a plate of hot biscuits on the table. "Eat up and give the cook a good name," she said.

"Who does he think he is?" he muttered. "Cap'n Bligh?"

"Never mind," said Lucy.

Finally everything was on the table. Geordie sat at

the head with the big tureen of steaming baked beans before him. Lucy sat at the foot. Geordie had been sitting in his father's chair since George Cameron had been
drowned while out hauling that August day. But her
mother's place was new to Lucy. An aunt had taken it
all the past week. She felt queer and shaky, and the
smell of food made her slightly sick.

Everyone was silent, as if waiting. Then Geordie
cleared his throat and said, "Whose turn is it?"

"Mine," said Peter. He folded his hands on the edge
of the table and bowed his red head, and the others all did
the same. "Dear God, thank you for all this good food
we have to eat, beans and pickles and biscuits and cur-
rant jelly, and—" he opened one eye, surveyed the table
—"and cole slaw and milk, and—" there were loud sighs
and shifting feet—"and everything," he finished rapidly.
"Oh, I forgot the apple pie because it's not on the table,
but thank you for that too. Amen."

"You don't have to read Him the catalogue," Penn
said. "He knows what we've got to eat."

"Marm always says we don't thank God enough for
things, so I thought—" he stopped short and his eyes
flooded.

"Here." Hastily Genie took a plate of food from
Geordie and set it in front of Peter.

Everyone ate with good appetite, in spite of their sadness. There was pleasure in having the house to themselves again. And they'd all worked hard that Saturday.
Geordie had hauled two hundred and fifty lobster traps.
Lucy and Genie had worked in the house and at gathering what was left in the garden. The twins had collected

apples in the old orchard. Penn had dug six hods of clams on the low tide early that morning, and then played high-school football in the afternoon.

No one talked at first, but on the second helpings conversation began by fits and starts, everyone taking part but Penn, who was still sulking. For Lucy it was an effort to talk of casual things, and she knew Geordie had to work hard at it too. But it was part of their job as the new heads of the family. She wondered how her mother had managed to seem so calm and cheerful for so long after her husband died. It must have been a relief when pneumonia struck her down and she didn't have to act out a part anymore.

It's bad enough for us, Lucy thought, but it was worse for her. And she thought of Scott, and wondered how it would be to love anyone so much that you had no will to live without him. . . .

"Excuse me, please," Penn said, getting up.

"Where are *you* going?" Geordie said.

"I'm going into town for a while."

"Not tonight you aren't. We've got things to talk about."

"What things?"

"I don't figger on going into it right now," said Geordie. Blue eyes struck sparks from blue eyes.

"Oh, my gosh," Genie wailed, "I was going to the library tonight to help Ralph on his history assignment! I *promised* him, and Lucy said I could."

"We don't need you at the meeting," Geordie said. "Penn can take you in and come right back."

"Oh, good!" Radiant, she began to hurry clearing the

table. At fourteen and a half she was still boy-thin in most places. She and Lucy were both tall and long-legged. They had the same warm coloring, the same dark auburn hair, the fine Sylvester features, the brown Sylvester eyes from a French ancestor.

"You don't have to do dishes tonight if you want to get going," Lucy said.

"You're a doll!" Genie rushed upstairs to change her clothes.

"Look," said Penn, "if it's what I think it is, what's there to talk about? Let 'em go, that's what I say. They'll have more than we ever had, and———"

"*Penn,*" said Lucy sharply. Fortunately the twins were talking to each other and Harold, and hadn't heard.

"Why can't I hang around town till the library closes and bring Genie home? Then we can talk."

"Because the session is to be between you, Lucy, and me," said Geordie with a patience that was a warning in itself. Penn turned abruptly and went out. In a few minutes Genie came running downstairs, carrying an armful of books.

"So long, everybody!" she called on her way through.

"Hey, can we ride in with Penn?" Philip asked.

"You can ride up to bed," said Lucy. "I know it's early, but you've had a long day and you can hardly see straight now."

"We won't go to bed!" the child lashed out. "We *hate* that old room!" He burst into tears and when Lucy reached for him he fought her with his fists. Peter, his own face twisted up in sympathy, ran into the front hall.

10

Geordie reached out and plucked the flailing Philip away from Lucy.

"Come on, old boy," he said, steering Philip after Peter. "I'll go up with you." Poor little devils, he thought as he followed the two slight figures up the stairs, listening to Philip's angry sobs and Peter's sniffling. They'd never been *sent* to bed in their lives until this week. Marm had let them race around indoors and out until all hours.

"Childhood's for having fun," Pa used to say. "Soon enough they'll be having to turn in when it's dark under the table so they'll be ready for the job by morning."

"What about school?" Geordie had asked him once when it had been impossible to get them up in time.

"Now, son," Pa said, "don't you think it's a crime to shut young ones up in school in this weather?"

"Ayuh," said Geordie. "Always did, but it never struck me you were of that way of thinking, back when I was their age."

"Well, a man should loosen up a bit as he gets older. Be a lot less rigid."

Geordie followed the boys into their room and put on the light. They began silently to undress. Geordie had never seen them into bed before, and now he was oddly moved by the skinny arms and legs and the delicate backs of their necks. He looked around the cluttered, busy room of two small boys. The slant of the ceiling ran almost to the floor, and one long window looked out over the cove. He wondered what else they could start collecting; he had no doubt that they could squeeze quite a few more objects in among the arrowheads, cars, and horseshoe-crab shells.

The boys were in their pajamas now, their dungarees and shirts folded neatly on chairs. Maybe they remembered how Geordie had always threatened them, "If I had my way, you boys would move, and no back talk."

And Marm had always been there to say, "Never mind, boys. Geordie won't tan you. He was only fooling."

"Well!" he said heartily. "That was quick. Climb in, now."

They dived into bed as if to escape him. Suddenly Philip turned his face hastily into his pillow, and Peter flung an arm across his eyes. Geordie stood over the bed. "What's the matter? Don't you feel good? You sick anywhere?" God, don't let them be sick, he prayed frantically. We've had enough sickness around here for a while. . . . He laid his palm on Peter's forehead. It was warm, but it didn't seem too much so.

"We ain't sick," whispered Peter. "But it's awful lonesome. Marm used to be down in the kitchen singing and rocking when we went to sleep."

Geordie had to clear his throat before he could speak. "Move over next to Pip," he said to Peter, "and I'll lie down awhile with you. I feel kind of lonesome myself." He kicked off his moccasins.

Peter's smile was instantaneous. "Get in the middle," he said, rising up out of the way. With Geordie stretched out between them, Philip still lay with his face in the pillow, and Geordie pulled him close.

"He feels awful," said Peter. "We think maybe God

took Marm and Pa because we didn't mind them very good. But they never seemed to worry about it, so we didn't think He would."

"You come here too," ordered Geordie, hugging Peter to him. "Let me put you straight on this, fellers. Pa had an accident when he was trying to get that rope out of his wheel, and he couldn't save himself, so God took him. And Marm had to go because—well, she wasn't very happy around here without Pa, even with all of us. And he'd be just about lost without her."

"Even in Heaven?" asked Peter incredulously.

"Even in Heaven. But they know we can all take care of each other."

"But you have to make all the money," Peter said, "and lobstering's not very good these days. I know one thing *we* can do. We won't eat so much, so it won't take so much money to feed us."

"You're going to eat all I can get for you," Geordie said hoarsely. "But there's other ways you can help." If he didn't get out of here he was going to be bawling himself in a minute. He gave Philip a hard hug. "You listening, Pip?"

Philip said unexpectedly, "We can help Lucy more, and mind Genie better."

"Genie's awful bossy," said Peter, not willing to concede too much.

"I'll talk to her," Geordie promised.

"You know what you're always saying when you feel good, Geordie?" Philip asked. "You know that thing you yell? Well, what's it mean?"

"Why, it means like when you say to company, Come

in and sit down. Only it's to do with being aboard a boat, and somebody comes rowing across to visit you."

"Couldn't it mean there ain't nothing to worry about? That's what you make it sound like when you say it. Only you ain't said it for a long time."

"Ayuh," chimed in Peter. "Say it now, so we'll know everything's going to be all right!"

"Lemme get squared away here then," said Geordie, and got up. Standing in the middle of the room he threw back his head and gave the hail his father had taught him, as he himself had been taught by *his* father, who'd been a Grand Banks fisherman.

"Come a-bo-oard and bring your do-o-ry!"

"That's it!" cried Peter. "Gee, Pip, don't that sound like a real old Indian war whoop or something?"

Philip bounced up, laughing and hugging his knees.

"For heaven's sake!" Lucy called. "What's going on in there?"

"Don't you tell her, Geordie," said Peter. "Let her guess. Does girls good to guess."

"You fellers are catching on too quick," said Geordie.

"There's the truck," Philip said suddenly. "Penn's back. Now you can have your meeting."

"You two be all right now? Not quite so lonesome?"

"Nope." Peter yawned. "Guess you can put out the light."

Geordie rumpled each head lightly, put out the light, and went downstairs. Lucy met him at the foot.

"Are they all right?" she asked in a low voice.

"They're as all right as any of us are," he said. "Nobody knows about tomorrow. You should have called

14

Scott up and had a night out with him, even if it wasn't any more than a ride and a lobster roll somewhere. You haven't seen much of him lately, and if he gets drafted you'll see even less."

"I've seen as much of him as you've seen of Donna," she retorted. "What's the matter with *you* having a night out?"

"Plenty of time for that when we get straightened out. She understands that."

"So does Scott. He's so darned good that way. And we're trying not to think about him going away." Her smile was luminous. "Maybe next week we could all four of us go to the dance. You think anybody'd criticize us?"

"Not if we don't get drunk," said Geordie, straight-faced.

2

PENN was in the kitchen, having another piece of pie. "Well, I delivered Genie to Little Lord Fauntleroy on the library steps," he said. After a moment he added, "I saw Donna too. I didn't recognize the car she was in. Or the guy driving it."

Geordie gave no sign of noticing, but Lucy felt like kicking Penn under the table. "Good pie," he said to her with a mischievously sweet smile. *You watch yourself,* her lips warned him. She cut pie for herself and Geordie, and made instant coffee.

"Well, Penn," Geordie said finally, "you thought any more about what colleges you'll try for?"

"Yep. I'm trying for none. It was never *my* idea, it was always theirs, you know that."

"So the minute they're gone, you're through with it." Geordie's eyes were hard. "That shows just how much you thought of them."

Penn's face went dark red, and he half-rose. Lucy said quickly, "That's not fair, Geordie."

"All right, maybe I shouldn't have said it. I'm sorry,"

he said gruffly. "Sit down again. Listen, did it ever occur to you maybe it'd be a fine thing to do for the rest of us? This bunch that's been around here all week—they all acted as if Marm'd married beneath her. As if none of us could get anywhere on our own because we're too much Cameron. Well, our great-grampa Cameron was a famous minister and head of a big college, remember. He had one degree from Edinburgh University and another from Oxford, and more besides."

"Let's face it, brother mine," said Penn. "Those days are gone forever. They went when Pa's old man ran away from all that education and ended up fishing for cod from a dory on the Grand Banks. We're just run of the mill now and maybe a little less than that. One college degree in this gang isn't going to make us respected overnight."

"They respect us now, Penn," Lucy said. "They know Pa was a good man and Marm a good woman, and none of us have ever been in any trouble. But Geordie means——"

"I can tell him what I mean," said Geordie. "We're going to do the best we can with whatever we've got. Even those two up there—" he glanced at the ceiling— "have been trying to figger what *they* can do. Lucy's the finest kind of a housekeeper, and I'm a pretty good lobsterman and hoping to be a better one. Genie's a kid yet, and with her we don't know yet which way the cat's going to jump. But you're supposed to have the family brains. And you're going to use 'em to get into college."

"Colleges like money." Penn was sarcastic, but he was nervously biting the inside of his cheek.

17

"I've only been out of high school since last June, Penn," Lucy said. "I remember about the scholarships and the government loans. Mr. Gardner said——"

"Don't quote that kook to me. I spend my days dodging him."

"What's the matter with you?" Geordie asked, too quietly. "I know darn well you aren't lazy. Not with your hands, anyway. But when it comes to using your head you act just about as shiftless as old Jud Pearse."

"Jud's not so stupid," Penn retorted. "He goes his own pace, and he knows the town won't let him starve or go cold in the wintertime."

"Is that what *you* want?" Geordie stood up, and Harold barked. Lucy felt her heart jump, and she pulled hard at Geordie's rigid arm.

"Careful . . . don't shout . . . the kids," she said breathlessly.

Penn's voice was low but savage. "Can't you get it through your head I'm sick of school? Just because I can do the work doesn't mean I'm crazy about it. I've been sick of school for a long time. You think I want to stick out my neck for four years more of it and then owe my soul till it's paid back, tied up in some high-priced job where I can never be free again? Not me!"

He began pacing around the kitchen. "The folks didn't have to go before I made up my mind. I did that a long time ago, and I was going to get it over to 'em somehow. . . . Only Pa had that bug about the educated Camerons, and Marm wanted to show her folks that Pa came of good stock, and so they had me in a cleft stick."

18

"Strikes me," said Geordie slowly, "that any thought of responsibility to the rest of us makes you feel caught in a cleft stick."

Penn laughed harshly. "You're lying in your teeth, chummy, if you say you don't feel caught in a cleft stick yourself! But you won't admit it. You're too darn self-righteous. You think a thunderbolt'll strike you dead if you're honest for once!" Before Geordie could answer he rushed on. "I'm responsible for myself, that's all. I'll get my diploma. I'll do that much. And then I'll be on my own. *Free,* outside four walls."

"Till the Army gets you," said Geordie.

Penn stared at him. "I'm not scared of that. I just may enlist. But I'll still be on my own . . . only you can't see that, can you? You two could be free too, if you didn't have all these pious ideas. You could get married, if that's what you want. *I* don't, but you've both got steadies—" he grinned—"I don't know how steady, after tonight."

"Stop that cheap talk," Lucy said. Her mouth was dry, and it wasn't because of the insinuation about Geordie's Donna.

"Look, Luce." Penn appealed to her. "You think I don't love the little kids. Of course I do, for Pete's sake! But what have we got for them here? You could do 'em more harm than good by hanging onto them. Look what Bill Sylvester could do for the twins! And they'd probably go to college, if you're so set on that. So how can you deprive them of it? I'm telling you, you'd better let them go before the town steps in and does the parceling out."

Lucy gasped. Hardly moving his lips Geordie said, "You disposed of Genie too?"

"I'll bet the Sylvesters would take her if you'd let them have the twins. She'd be a help, and she'd get a good education, and see something else besides spruce trees and Ralph."

The new lines in Geordie's face looked as deep as scars. "I never thought I'd ever hear anything like this coming out of a Cameron. You really believe that strangers can make it up to those kids for losing their whole family at one whack?"

"Sure," said Penn, "because I'm a realist. My talent for realism is my prized possession."

"Oh?" said Geordie dryly. "I thought *you* were. You got any schoolwork for Monday?"

"Chemistry exam. I'd better get at it."

"Tell me something, Penn," said Lucy. "If you feel the way you do about school, why bother to work for good marks?"

"I told you I'd get my diploma and I'm in line for vale-dictory," he said angrily. "I won't just squeeze by. I'll do that much for——" *For them,* he had almost said. Geordie got up abruptly and walked out, yanking his jacket off the hook on the way. Harold sprang after him.

"I'll pick up Genie," Geordie said without looking back. "Want to ride in, Luce?" He kept on going.

"I've got all these dishes——"

"The devil with 'em. I'll help you myself, after-wards."

"Who am I to turn that down?" she said, but he was already outside, talking to Harold. Lucy got her coat.

Penn said, "Well, I suppose my ears'll burn clean off now."

"Don't worry, we won't talk about you," she said coldly, then relented. "But darn it all, Penn, that was a terrible thing to say about the kids! As if we should leap at the chance to give them away like puppies, so we can be free!"

"So they can have more," he corrected her.

"But you said the other thing first, so that's what you thought of first." Suddenly she wanted to cry, she wanted her father and mother, she wanted Scott. She ran out to where the truck was waiting, the motor running, and climbed in. Harold sat up very tall beside Geordie. In transports of joy at the thought of a ride, he met Lucy with tumultuous kisses, and in the confusion she got safely past another awful moment of weakness.

3

G EORDIE'S silence was a grim fourth passenger all
the way up the lane through the spruce woods
to the black road. By the time the pickup rocked
around the turn by their mailbox Lucy couldn't keep
quiet any longer. Harold sat importantly between them,
watching the road as if their safe navigation depended on
him. So she used him as an opener.

"Where'll we put Genie? Harold can't ride alone in
back. He'll be jumping out and taking off by himself. I
guess I'll have to sit with him."

"I'll do that, and you can drive," said Geordie. "I
dunno but what Harold's the most restful company a
man could find right now. Oh, you're all right too," he
added roughly.

"Thanks, or should I bark it? . . . Listen, Geordie,
you ought to know Penn by now. That's the way he felt
about college today. It's got nothing to do with next
week. He's got another month before he has to get his
applications in, so why don't we just leave him alone,
and——"

"He's spoiled rotten," said Geordie. "That's why he's

got such a big idea of himself. Look at the way he was brought up."

"Marm and Pa were never mean to *us!*" Lucy protested.

"No, they were good, but strict too. You had spankings, I had spankings, but did any of the young ones, ever? *No.* And no chores unless they offered to do 'em. And Penn was treated like a little prince when he started bringing home those good rank cards and reading fourth-grade books before he was hardly out of the first. Pa would listen to Penn explaining the solar system like it was Holy Writ, and Marm had him reading aloud while she ironed, but let me try to explain why we should put the spare dollars into more gear instead of that set of encyclopedias, and Pa thought I was jealous."

Lucy sensed the hurt under his harsh tone. He went on, "And then he can stand there tonight and all but laugh at them for thinking he was so smart. That's what goweled me, Luce. He grabbed all the attention, got away with no chores because his homework was so important, and now he's laughing at them for it."

"Oh, Geordie, I don't believe that!" Lucy hugged Harold extra hard in her emotion, and he gave her a protesting lick on the ear. "Maybe he was telling the truth tonight when he said he'd been trying to get out of it for a long time. You know how Pa was when he had his heart set on anything, he just couldn't hear anything else. Penn might have hated chores, but he's not lazy at jobs he gets for himself. He's bought his own clothes for a long time now."

"Ayuh, and once in a while he'd give the old folks a

few dollars, out of the goodness of his heart." Geordie was sarcastic. "Well, if he doesn't start thinking about college his days as Bonnie Prince Charlie around our house are numbered. He'll be a commoner like the rest of us."

Lucy had to laugh. "Oh, but wouldn't he look gorgeous in a kilt, though? And you too. As the head of the family you'd be known as The Cameron."

After a minute he laughed too. As the first lights of Port George showed, Harold stood up panting loudly in anticipation. "Sit down, Harold," said Geordie. "You think Penn may go ahead with it then?"

"If we don't keep telling him he should. He resents that, and it's only natural. We're not much older than he is."

"Well, I'll make a mighty effort to keep my mouth shut."

"What bothered me more," said Lucy, "was something he said about the town taking the kids." She spoke fast, to tumble it out before they reached the library.

"He was just trying to bug you," Geordie said. "Mr. Bartlett told me that as long as the kids didn't miss school, didn't get into trouble, had enough to eat and enough to wear, I can be made their legal guardian when I'm twenty-one."

"And you'll be twenty-one next February," she said. "You and George Washington."

"You mean Geordie Washington, don't ye?"

Lucy relaxed against the seat. She'd forgotten what the First Selectman had told them. Now she felt, if not

24

exactly happy, at least reassured, the way the twins had looked after Geordie roared out, "Come aboard and bring your dory!" And now she knew why he had done it.

They were on Main Street now, and Harold stood up again, breathing hard. "For the love of Mike, sit down and stop fogging up the windshield," said Geordie. "And your tail's beating my ear off!"

"Mine too," said Lucy, getting a practiced hammerlock on Harold and forcibly sitting him down again. They drove past the lighted windows of pleasant houses and under high-arching elms. There were more lights at the harbor, where two huge trucks loaded lobsters at the Barstow & Cady Lobster Company for the long ride to New York and beyond. A big herring carrier headed down the length of the harbor toward the sardine factory, which was brightly illuminated and ready to start processing a fresh load.

Lucy had worked at the factory for two summer vacations from high school, earned all her clothes for school, and had paid board to help out at home. She had planned to work there full time after she graduated, to help get things she'd need when she and Scott got married. Now she was an unpaid housekeeper.

"Not that I'd have it any different," she told herself fiercely now. "I wouldn't let anybody else do my job. Scott won't mind if we have to wait a little longer. It's *me*. Sometimes it seems like we'll have to wait forever."

Her throat hurt with the ache of held-back tears. She wanted Marm and Pa back, not just so she could marry

Scott soon, but because they were Marm and Pa. Without them the family was—well, like Harold if he suddenly lost a leg and couldn't go racing across the rocks anymore trying to catch a seagull.

The pickup stopped at the little Cape Cod house that was the town library. Genie and Ralph Morey sat on the brick steps that led between the barberry hedge from the lawn to the pavement. They got up and came to the truck, and Harold lunged across Geordie and thrust his big head out at Genie, indicating with rapture that he hadn't seen her for a year.

"You kook," she told him fondly. "Kiss Ralph." Laughing, Ralph dodged the ardent tongue. Geordie got out, keeping a firm grip on the dog's collar, and ordered him into the back of the pickup, from which Harold leaned out whining and panting and swabbing unwary ears and napes.

Ralph was Genie's age, a short, compact boy with curly fair hair he tried to control by keeping it cropped short. He had a cheerful, open face with a snub nose and long eyelashes which he hated as much as his curls.

"Ralph's coming over tomorrow," said Genie, "and we're going to collect specimens for biology around the shore."

"If it's all right," Ralph interrupted. "Maybe I shouldn't." He looked worriedly from Geordie to Lucy.

"Why?" asked Geordie. "You figgering on salting down the kids for specimens? Sure you can come. What are you asking for? You never did before."

"All I meant," Ralph explained with dignity, "is that

26

maybe I shouldn't come over and bother after everything that's happened—you know——" He shifted his feet and waved his hands, not able to explain. Lucy took pity on him.

"You come along, Ralph," she said. "We've missed you. We can't have everything the same as it was, but we want to be as near natural as possible, and you're part of it."

"*Thanks!*" he said on a gusty breath of relief. "I've missed coming too. Hey, you know you're all lucky in one way? None of you is an only kid." Suddenly overcome with embarrassment he grabbed Harold, burrowed his face in the dog's neck and called him muffled, insulting, and affectionate names.

"Come on, break up the love scene," said Geordie. "I put in a long day's work even if nobody else does around here."

There were assorted good nights, and as the truck drove off Harold barked loudly for as long as he could still see Ralph standing back there under the streetlight. Then he put his cold nose on Geordie's cheek as if to make sure of him, sat down beside him, and leaned hard against his shoulder.

In the front seat Genie ran on about the evening's work. It was good to hear her enthusiastic tone. Lucy had heard her crying at night during the week, but they'd all had tears to shed, and the older ones had tried to keep them secret from the younger ones and from each other.

"I wish I had a bike," Genie said. "I could get a secondhand one if I had a little more money. I think maybe I'll advertise for baby-sitting jobs on the bulletin board in the store. . . . Can I?" she added a little uncertainly.

"We'll see. . . . If you got paid by the hour for all the help you've given Ralph, you could afford a brand-new bike."

"Oh, he helps me with my math, so it's a fair exchange."

The truck headed out of town along the deserted stretch of road. Lucy drove carefully in case a deer should suddenly leap out of the woods. "You know what, Luce?" Genie said. "I think Penn's got a girl! He always pretends he can't be bothered with just one, and he'd rather have them all fighting for dates with him. But Ralph told me Shelley Sears brought Penn home from the game in her car."

"That's no sign of anything. She goes to Limerock High, so does Penn. So do you. So did I, till last June."

"But he's been out with her other times, only they don't make anything of it. I mean they don't have dates in *public*. Ralph's seen them in her car. . . . You know how he's all over the place on his bike, exploring wood roads and everything. Well, one Sunday he went out to poke around the cellar holes on Heron Point, and they were parked out there. They didn't see him, they were too busy gazing into each other's eyes."

"Do you and Ralph study in the library, or gossip?"

"It's not gossip, when it's about your own family!" said Genie indignantly. "Aren't you interested? And when you think who she *is,* for heaven's sake!" She giggled. "Ralph calls her the 'erring 'eiress."

Lucy laughed too, but she was disturbed. She knew

Shelley only by sight, a thin, fair, rather shy-appearing girl who had been sent away to expensive boarding schools most of her life, and had spent her school vacations on trips with her mother. Her father owned the big sardine-packing plant and the fleet of carriers, and also controlled most of the seiners. He was a native of Port George, but his wife was a New Yorker who hated small-town life and loved traveling. Apparently Shelley had rebelled at boarding school this year, and insisted on staying in Port George and going to the regional high school at Limerock.

"Everybody likes Shelley," Genie was running on now. "At first they thought she was stuck-up because she was so quiet, but it's just the way she is. She's not much of a mixer, but she's nice."

Was Shelley the reason for Penn's violent refusal to try for college? Did he think by any wild chance that this rich girl would still be here after graduation next June? Her mother would probably take her off to Europe for the summer. Then she would be off to college somewhere herself, far away, and these few secret dates would be remembered as simple fun with a handsome local boy, and nothing more.

They were turning into their own road now. Lucy said, "Don't tell Geordie about this. He'll worry for fear Penn'll slack up on his schoolwork if he's got a girl."

"I won't say anything, but if Penn does slack off, Mr. Gardner will be on his neck. There's a full scholarship for Bowdoin he wants him to try for. Ralph told me that too."

"How the heck does Ralph find out all these things?"

"By accident," said Genie smugly. "He's not a sneak, if that's what you think. He had to go to the office yesterday, and he heard Mr. Gardner talking to Mr. Price about it. Ralph thought it was great. He thinks we Camerons are some smart."

Lucy felt better again, knowing that the vocational guidance counselor and the principal weren't ready to give up on Penn. But these seesaw reactions at the end of a hard day were making her sick.

"I hope Geordie and Harold are still with us," she said lightly. "Wouldn't it be awful if they'd flown out of the truck and into the bushes when we hit that last hole?"

~~~~~~

T HE SEA was as calm and blue as the old ice pond. Along the shores some autumn color still flamed amid the dark stands of spruce. The sun was warm. Geordie had twenty-five new traps set, and the old ones were doing him proud since he'd gone over the whole batch, replacing weak laths and trapheads.

The weather had been mostly fine for a couple of weeks now, and here it was early November. He was grateful for each day of it. The old boat couldn't stand much in the way of pounding without loosening her seams and taking in water. It meant he'd lose days in the winter, when stronger boats could go.

"But if I get a good fall's work in," he'd told Lucy at their before-daylight breakfast that morning, "we'll get along all right this winter, even if I can only dodge out between windy spells." *If nobody gets sick* was the unspoken thought between them. They'd just finished paying what their mother's illness had cost them in dollars. Penn had helped on that, to give him credit. Marm's folks had paid for the funeral, to give *them* credit. Credit, but not the kids. Never the kids. Lucy had written polite letters of thanks for their help, and of refusal to their anxious offers, and the four older Camerons had all signed. Penn had been sulky about it, but he'd written his name.

Georgie saw one of his blue-and-yellow buoys ahead, slowed down and gaffed it. The hauling gear droned as it dragged the trap out of the water. He thought with brief longing of the modern hydraulic haulers that snapped the traps up and aboard in a few seconds. Never mind, as long as this one worked and he had the strength in his arms and shoulders to heave the traps up onto the washboard. . . . Three big lobsters in this one. He allowed himself a small grin, not big enough to tempt Fate.

Other boats worked on the broad, shimmering blue bay. Most were a lot newer than *Mary C.*, and equipped with fathometers and radio telephones. They'd be able to go all winter except when the gales howled along the coast. Geordie wanted winter lobstering, when the price could run up to a dollar and a half a pound. He wanted a strong boat and a big marine engine. He wanted——

He was letting himself go, as bad as the kids with the mail-order catalogue, the "wish book." But by godfrey mighty, he'd have some kind of decent boat before another fall. Maybe not brand-new, but new to him. And for now, just let this kind of lobstering and weather keep up through December, and they'd actually be able to put some money away this winter. He could spend a few dollars on taking Donna out now and then, without feeling guilty. He allowed himself to dream a little as he headed for the next trap, not of a new boat next year, but of Donna with her fine bones and her small waist, her soft, chuckling laughter, her honey-colored eyes. He could be poetic about Donna without anyone's knowing it. Lucy had said once that Donna was born knowing how to be a woman. And she was his girl. Even after a year he could hardly believe it sometimes.

He had a little way to run now to his next gang of traps, and he had a cup of coffee and a ham sandwich. His food was beginning to taste good to him once more. Penn had been really hitting the books, the twins actually wanted to help him around the fishhouse, and yesterday they'd done a good job of baiting up for him. Genie was a good kid anyway.

Now he was heading toward the little group of islands called the Nuggets. His father had always kept traps there, and got his best lobsters from the rich kelpy bottom around the remains of wharves where long ago other men had lived in camps and gone lobstering. Most of the camps had fallen down among the wild roses and baybushes. Burt Watson, who had inherited the Nuggets, had never lived out there, and didn't care who set traps among the islands.

That was one time in his life when Pa was lucky, Geordie mused. Being the one to fish the Nuggets. It was here that Geordie had set his twenty-five new traps, two days ago, and he expected them to practically pay for themselves in the first haul.

Sea ducks feeding in the lee flew away before the oncoming boat as he entered the shining avenues of water winding among steep terraces of rock. But where were his blue-and-yellow buoys? Strange red-and-white ones floated on the shimmering surface—but none of his. Incredulously he slowed his engine and scanned waters on shore.

There was one at last, too close to the rocks. He eased the boat in, gaffed the buoy, and hauled the trap aboard. It was empty, and the door was open; the familiar warning to get out. Used on *him,* in his own berth.

His heart seemed to be crashing around in his chest. This kind of rage was almost as bad as grief. He had to swallow to ease his throat, and the sun scalded his eyes as he went scavenging among the islets looking for the rest of his buoys. He found several floating free, cut off, and two more traps that had been hauled and left with the doors open. Of the other twenty-two, there was no sign.

He felt murderous. The loss would have been bad any time, but right now, with winter coming on and a hundred dollars making all the difference between saving something and going behind—he pounded his clenched fist on the washboard and cursed the destroyer. Then he gaffed the next red-and-white buoy as if he were hooking its owner.

The name burned into the wood was as strange as the buoys. "M. Tolman." Not a Port George name; he'd never seen it before. Instinctively he looked across at Gold, the biggest of the Nuggets. The camp on it was in pretty good condition, because Burt Watson's grandchildren used it in summer. Now Geordie saw a thread of smoke going into the air.

A squatter. He must have moved in yesterday because there'd been nobody the day before. Geordie grinned fiercely at the red-and-white buoy lying on the washboard. "Well, M. Tolman," he said aloud, "here's where you get a little of your own back."

He picked up his knife. The thought of revenge was as sweet as spring water after a long thirst. He'd cut off every red-and-white buoy he could find; well, at least twenty-two. And he'd haul three to make up for his three that had been robbed of their catch but not cut off.

One swipe with the knife, and he'd be off to a good start. The only trouble was, Pa was in the way. He might just as well be standing there, talking between puffs on the old corncob pipe, Geordie could hear him so clearly.

"Getting even's a waste of time and effort. Besides, it makes you no better'n the feller who's wronged you."

"Pa, we aren't talking about the time Charlie stole my Christmas jackknife," Geordie argued in his head. "Sure, you were right then. But this is different. It's our living! I got that trap stock on credit, and I've got those kids to feed and clothe, and I have to count on fishing the Nuggets because when it gets real bad weather the boat can't go far outside, old as she is."

"Thievery's thievery, no matter what. We're Camerons, we don't do such things."

"I never thought Camerons were willing to go on the town, either!" Geordie snarled. He flung the buoy overboard and started up the engine. "All right. I'll compromise. I'll make sure he's the one who did it, and *then* I'll cut."

But there was no boat tied up at the rickety spile dock on Gold, though there were traps piled on it. They were a poor lot compared to the big handsome four-headers the squatter had cut off. The smoke still trickled from the camp chimney like a sly grin of mockery. A black cat watched him from a boulder as he cruised slowly by.

Leaving the shelter of the islands he headed into choppy waters. The slap of water along the boat's sides and her up-and-down motion reminded him of the winter winds to come. This morning he'd been full of confidence, but now, depressed, he was sure that the fine weather was over and he was beaten before he'd even had a good start. He did fairly well out of the traps he had around the Whaleback along with several other men, but this didn't cheer him up. Only the thought of revenge could lift his spirits.

When he went into Port George, a strange boat passed him, heading out of the harbor and toward the Nuggets. She was a low dirty-gray thirty-footer, with an old-fashioned fantail stern and an open cockpit half covered with a stained canvas sprayhood. A sneaking tramp of a boat, he thought. The man at the wheel *had* to be M. Tolman, squatter and thief. Wait till Monday morning, Cap'n Tolman, Geordie thought.

Sam Cady, buyer for Barstow & Cady, noticed the traps on the stern. "What's the matter with them?"

"Oh, they're not fishing the way they should," said Geordie. "Maybe it's the way they're rigged. I'm going to reset the heads."

"Fussy, ain't ye? Well, it pays to take pains. Feels like you're doing all right though," he said as they swung the second heavy crate onto the scales. "The fall spurt's hanging on." He grinned and said out of the side of his mouth, "Don't look now, but you're being sketched. Feller up on the wharf been drawing the picturesque natives all afternoon."

Geordie turned his head away deliberately and stared down the harbor.

"Don't be uncivil, boy." Sam moved the weights. "Give him and his girl a treat. You're the first young one to come in except Willy Tuttle, and he's about two hundred and fifty pounds too picturesque."

"Speaking of picturesque, was there a scrubby old antique of a boat just in here?"

"Not here, but I saw her. Went down to the factory. He had barrels aboard, so I guess he was after herring cuttings. They must be short of bait somewhere."

"You know if Burt Watson's sold the Nuggets, or renting?"

"Not that I know of, unless he's done it long distance from Boston. He's been up there a month, visiting his daughter." Sam's eyes were sharp and bright amid the weathered creases. "That boat got any connection?"

"I dunno." Geordie was carefully casual. "Smoke coming out of the chimney, that's all. I wondered."

"You being crowded?" the buyer asked alertly.

"Plenty of room out there. . . . Say, what about that cousin of Burt's, or whatever he was? Somebody down east? I heard my father say once that Old Cap'n Watson left the place to the two of 'em when they were kids."

"Oh, I heard something once years ago, about some relations down Jonesport way selling everything out and going to Puget Sound. Likely sold it to Burt, if it's true." Sam shrugged. "I might not even remember the straight of it, it was so long ago." Two more boats were coming in, so Geordie tied *Mary C.* out of the way and went up the ramp to the wharf. Lucy had given him a grocery list.

His rubber boots felt cruelly heavy, and the ache in the back of his neck had nothing to do with his day's work. He had often felt it there when he was in a bad mood, but lately it hadn't been around much. Till today.

At the top of the ramp he veered around the gasoline pumps, and almost walked into a girl. There was a moment of consternation on both sides, in which he fought to keep from growling, "Why don't you look where you're going?"

Then he had the horrifying thought that he might have said it aloud, from her startled expression. She had a narrow tanned face with gray eyes under black eyebrows that lifted toward the temples, and springy short-cut hair as black as his own.

"Excuse me," he said.

"Certainly," she said, just as distantly. He walked past the man on the crate, who looked up with a friendly nod.

"Hello! Great day, isn't it?"

"Fine day," said Geordie, and went on. The man had a short gray beard and a beret. Gorry, he was a lot older than his girl friend. Well, it took all kinds. He and Donna——

The name flew across his tormented spirit like a bright bird above a turbulent sea. He forgot the odd couple on

38

the wharf, he forgot the attack on his gear. Donna would be home from her job in Limerock now. She got out at four.

Instead of going up the dirt road to Main Street, he swung off onto a path that followed around the harbor shore almost to the outermost point. Here a pleasant white house sat snug against tall spruces, facing the harbor mouth. Donna's father was skipper of a herring carrier, and having his house out here was the next best thing to living aboard a boat. A town road went past the back of the house and out to the lighthouse, but in front he had rocks and surf aplenty.

Geordie hadn't had a chance to be with Donna since Marm was taken sick. They'd talked on the telephone some, and she told him she understood how things would be until they'd all got shaken down into the new way of doing things. Then, when at last he'd suggested a Saturday night dance at the Grange Hall with Scott and Lucy, she'd been all flustered. Seemed she'd promised a friend they'd do each other's hair that night. So Georgie had stayed home with the kids, but the next morning when he drove them in to Sunday school he'd gone around to the Blake place.

Someone was humming in the kitchen now as he reached the screen door. If it was Donna he was going to take her in his arms and hold her tight, even if he was in his work clothes. His nose tickled pleasantly in anticipation of that silky, flyaway fair hair. He tapped on the screen, grinning.

"Just a minute!" *Mrs. Blake. Never mind, Donna*

was somewhere in the house. He kept on smiling at the pretty wide-eyed woman, who looked at him as if he were the Grim Reaper in person.

"Hello, Mrs. Blake. Donna home yet?"

"Oh . . . Geordie!" One hand fluttered against her breast. "What are *you* doing here at this time of day, dear?"

"I came in to sell, thought I'd walk around and catch her, that's all." Why didn't she ask him in? She was red as one of her dahlias, and this time the Cap'n wasn't home to ask what ailed her.

"Well, she isn't here, Geordie. She's . . . uh . . . staying uptown and having supper with someone she knows at the bank, and . . . uh . . . going to the movies."

"Oh." Geordie fought to hide his disappointment. "Well, that's all right. Good for her. Thanks, Mrs. Blake." He turned to go, and he had almost reached the gate when she bleated softly after him, *"Geordie!"*

He turned sharply. She said, "Geordie dear, I don't think you'd better come anymore. It's—well, she's very *young* for her years, and her father says she's flighty, but . . . well, her attention *strayed,* you see, while you were so busy——"

He could hardly believe what he was hearing. He felt as if there were nothing left of him but his clothes standing up there like a scarecrow. All gone. His brain, his insides, everything.

"You do understand, dear, don't you?" she was asking anxiously. "Her father and I think the *world* of you.

. . . You're so steady and mature. But Donna—well——"

"Thanks, Mrs. Blake. I appreciate you telling me."

He walked away. He didn't know how a scarecrow could feel sick, but he did. All those digs and prods from Penn that he'd ignored, thinking they were just Penn's deviltry. They weren't. Penn knew, Penn had seen.

Well, now *I* know, Geordie thought. And he went faster, not daring to think about her for fear he would hate her.

~~~~~~

5

ABOUT the time when Geordie was walking away from the Blake house, Lucy went out to take in the wash. She hoped Geordie had enjoyed his day's work as much as she'd enjoyed hers. It was queer to feel these sudden stabs of happiness when sorrow had stunned them for so long, but she just couldn't help it. The sea and sky were bluer than Grandmother Sylvester's blue porcelain bowl from China; the long shadows were a different blue, rich and deep, and when you walked through them they were cool as water, and then you came out into the warm gold light again.

She folded the sheets as she took them down, and laid them carefully in the basket. Robins and bluejays talked about old fallen fruit around the apple trees and a squirrel sat on a stump holding a piece of apple in his paws, and ate it very neatly. He was brave because Harold had gone up to the mailbox to wait for the school bus.

Lucy sang in the clear, true Cameron voice as she worked. It was Friday night again; pea soup was simmering on the stove, made with a good big ham bone; she was going out dancing with Scott tomorrow night, and it might be a double date. She'd know when Geordie came home. Donna hadn't been able to go out last Saturday night. Penn and his mischief! He probably saw Donna with her father, if he saw her at all.

She went on singing *On Wings of Song,* which she'd learned in Glee Club at school. Though nobody ever waltzed at any of the dances she and Scott went to, and even the twist was considered practically Civil War period, whenever she thought of going dancing with Scott she always saw herself waltzing with him, his arm around her waist, his hand holding hers firmly, and they were going round and round on a polished floor to this dreamy, romantic music. . . .

Noise exploded in the lane. The twins' shouts and Harold's barks echoed back and forth between the walls of spruces. The squirrel left. The twins appeared, leaping over each other's shadows, in a private twin-game they had, jumping up for low branches. Harold ran just for the fun of it. Behind them Ralph and Genie came, faces turned toward each other in absorbed conversation, Genie's books clasped to her chest while Ralph carried a load under each arm.

"Hey, Luce! We're hungry!" The twins and Harold headed for the house.

"Listen, you two!" she called. "Don't you help yourselves! I'll be right in!"

In the kitchen she made thick peanut-butter sandwiches and poured milk. Her mother had never restricted the raids on the pantry, but the twins could go through almost a whole loaf of bread and a full jar of peanut butter in an hour. Lucy found she was saving a couple of dollars a week by limiting them, and it still didn't deprive the children.

"No use to act like gulls," she told them now. "You know where your next meal's coming from, so you don't have to gulp down everything in sight in one fell swoop."

"You mean one swell foop, don't you?" asked Philip, and they fell over each other in hysterical delight.

"Boy, are *you* a gart smuy!" Peter gasped, and they collapsed again.

They went up to their room shouting nonsense at each other through mouthfuls of peanut-butter sandwich.

Harold drank noisily from his dish and knocked it around in demand for a refill. Ralph and Genie came in, Ralph carrying all the books and Genie the laundry basket with the rest of the wash folded neatly.

"Hi, Luce," said Ralph with a trusting grin, dumping his load on the table. "Genie invited me to supper. Is that all right?"

"I seem to recollect something about you and pea soup and johnnycake," said Lucy. "It's all right with me if it is with your mother. You'd better call her." She nodded toward the telephone and Ralph said, "I'll do it later. She wouldn't be home yet anyway. She's in the store this afternoon because Gladys had to go to the dentist." The Morey's owned the town's one drugstore.

"You want a peanut-butter and jelly sandwich, Ralph?" Genie said.

"Where's Penn?" Lucy asked.

"You don't think he'd lower himself to ride down from Limerock on the school bus with the lower classes, do you?" asked Genie, slathering margarine on bread.

44

"Oh, dearie me, *no!* Especially when his sister might speak disrespectfully to him. She might even *speak,* period."

"So where is he?" asked Lucy.

"Well, the last I saw of him he was heading out of the school grounds with Shelley," said Genie. "Maybe they've eloped. Anything to get out of college. Milk or coffee, Ralph?"

"Milk," said Lucy. "Both of you. What are you doing this afternoon?"

"We're going beachcombing around the point," said Ralph, "and see what's come ashore in those extra-high tides."

"You'll have help," Lucy warned them, "and I don't mean Harold."

"Gosh, I don't mind the kids," said Ralph. "I get a big boot out of them."

From upstairs a twin shouted, "Hey! Penn's driving a *car!*" They came thundering down the stairs, and Harold went into a frenzy of barking. Everybody rushed outside, to be dazzled by the vision of a Chevrolet hardtop painted a screaming fire-engine red, just coming to a stop where the road ended at the barn doors.

"Is that Shelley's car?" Lucy asked Ralph. With enchanted eyes on the Chevrolet, Ralph shook his head. "She's got a Mustang." He joined the excited group around the car.

Penn got out, trying not to grin but having to give way eventually. "Well, what do you think of her?"

"Wow!" said Ralph. "She's sure a good-looking job." The twins were stricken silent.

"Who does she belong to?" Lucy asked, with a horrid suspicion.

"Me," said Penn, as if she should have known. They stared at each other.

"You mean you want to buy her?" There was still hope.

"I've bought her," he said tersely. "From one of the guys at school. A Limerock kid. She's all paid for."

"Your college fund!" Genie gasped.

Penn's pleasure was gone, he was flushed and defensive. "I'm not going to college, and everybody around here knows it or ought to know it, so knock it off, will you?" He swung around on the others. "Stop getting fingerprints all over her. Don't let that dog jump up like that. He'll scratch the paint."

"Come here, Harold," said Genie coldly. "Don't you dare go near that thing. Penn's likely to shoot you."

"Pete, get out from behind the wheel," Penn snapped. "Don't touch anything in there!"

"What are you so crabby for?" Philip asked. "Give us a ride, huh, Penn?"

"I'm giving nobody a ride As soon as I clean up I'm going into town. I don't know when I'll be back." He stalked into the house.

"All right, kids," said Lucy, "don't touch the car until Penn invites you." The twins fell back, both fascinated and frustrated.

"Gosh, I wonder if he used up all his savings," said Genie. "He must have high-tailed it to the bank straight from school. Gosh, what'll Geordie say?"

"If you're going beachcombing you'd better get started," Lucy said. She sounded much more cheerful than she felt. So far Geordie had been willing to follow her advice about Penn, but how he could take this calmly she didn't know. She was all churned up herself, and her disposition was a lot easier than Geordie's.

"There's Geordie now!" Philip yelled.

"Oh, my judas!" Peter gasped with great drama. They pounded off down the path, yelling excuses at each other. "Gorry, he must have snuck in some old quiet. . . . I bet he shut the engine off and drifted in——"

"It's the first time they've missed being there to catch the lines and get his oilclothes and stuff," said Genie. She glared at the car. "All because of *that*."

"Heck, Genie, that's a darn nice car," Ralph objected.

"You mean it's better than a college education?" She transferred her glare to him and he said mildly, "Well, right now I'd rather have the car."

"You men are all alike," said Genie. "I'm sure *I'll* never ride in his old car if Harold's not welcome. Well, are we going or not?"

"Sure, but——"

She started for the shore and Ralph tramped after her, arguing all by himself.

Lucy went down toward the fishhouse. Geordie was coming up the wharf, arms full, his boots hitting the planks with hollow heavy thuds as if they weighed too much to lift clear. When the twins reached him, both talking at once, his expression didn't change as far as

Lucy could see. He handed Peter his oilclothes and Philip his lunchbox and water jug, and kept the carton of groceries.

Lucy met him at the head of the wharf. Silently they looked up to where the red car gleamed between the shabby old house and huge weathered barn.

"The playboy's at it again, huh?" Geordie said at last.

"I'm afraid so. He didn't say how much it was, but he bought it from another boy and it's all paid for. I don't know what it's done to his savings."

"Well, they're his savings," Geordie said. He looked tired tonight, the lines harsh again in a face too young for them.

"You got any coffee on? I need something hot in my innards. . . . Wish I was a drinking man."

"Oh, you don't either," said Lucy with an ever-watchful eye on the twins. "Camerons don't need liquor to brace them up. Geordie, I've been thinking off and on ever since Penn started fighting college. . . . Would it be so bad if he didn't go? I mean—there's worse things that could happen, and——"

"Listen, Luce," said Geordie, "I don't give a hoot in Hades whether he goes to college or not."

It was like a slap. She said crisply, "I'll run up and get the coffee started." As she hurried away she heard Philip say reverently, "Hey, Geordie, now we've got a car and a truck too. And hey, Geordie, it's a sixty-five!"

Geordie said nothing, and Lucy new that he was either so deeply disappointed in Penn that he couldn't let himself care anymore what the boy did, or something else

48

had happened that day to upset him so much that Penn's car didn't matter.

Donna? Maybe it wasn't just mischief on Penn's part. He kept saying things that Geordie didn't seem to hear, and which she'd tried to ignore. Maybe she should have questioned him.

Just before she reached the back door Penn came out in an aromatic cloud, his black hair glossily groomed, his shirt, cardigan, and slacks a symphony of matching hues. Mischievously she whistled and he glared at her, and then grinned. "Look, I want to duck out before Geordie lights into me. But tell the kids I'll give 'em a ride tomorrow, huh?"

"Genie won't go without Harold. You insulted him."

"Oh, Lord, I'll take him too." He ran past her toward the car, jingling the car keys in his hand, and she felt like calling after him, "Taking Shelley out?"

But she wasn't supposed to know about Shelley. He turned the car around in a rush and headed for the lane, giving Geordie an impudent toot and a wave on the way.

6

HOT COFFEE and a piece of gingerbread gave Geordie a little more color in his face, though it didn't break his silence, and he didn't eat as if he enjoyed it. He and the twins went back down to the shore again and he put *Mary C.* up beside the wharf on the high water, so that when the tide went out she would be high and dry. Tomorrow, Saturday, the twins were to help him paint her. They were talking about it very importantly when they came back, mercifully forgetting Penn's car for the time being.

Genie and Ralph came home under the first stars. Their feet and sleeves were wet with salt water, their hands were cold, and they reeked of the rockweed out of which they'd dragged planks and two-by-fours. They'd also brought home pockets full of interesting rocks, a strange old bottle, and one good oar. Penn didn't come home, of course, and Lucy wondered if he and Shelley were eating somewhere now, or driving through the clear blue-dark of early evening over the countryside. She felt both envy and understanding, sharp as pain. Penn had declared his freedom when his parents died; for her and Geordie the word had best be forgotten.

But not forever! she cried inside herself. It can't be forever! And her thoughts rushed to Scott and tomorrow night as if to a refuge, deliberately ignoring the fact that weekly they expected his draft summons. She couldn't dwell on that or she'd lose courage altogether.

After supper Ralph helped Genie with the dishes, then they went into the living room and Genie began picking out tunes on the old cottage organ. Their mother had taught her to read music, and the first tune from an old songbook summoned the twins.

Out in the kitchen Lucy sprinkled the ironing for tomorrow, and Geordie sat down to work on trapheads. "Listen," Lucy said as the chorus burst into a swinging version of *Showers of Blessings*. "If they can sing, they never even think of turning on the television. This winter I think we should sing more, and teach them more card games, and—" she took courage from the sound of her own voice—"we could read aloud on winter evenings. Do a lot more things so they don't think of that darned old TV."

Geordie didn't answer. She said, "What happened today?"

"Nothing."

"You're lying," she said.

"All right." He threw down the wooden shuttle and sat back in his chair. "I'll tell you, but if you lose sleep tonight about it, don't blame me."

He told her about the new traps sunk or destroyed out around the Nuggets. So it wasn't Donna—*yet*. She was relieved about that, but dismayed, outraged, and then worried about the vandalism.

"What are you going to do?" she asked. "Does the man have a right to be there in the first place?"

"I don't know. Sam Cady doesn't know him, and Burt's away in Boston. But it doesn't seem like him to rent the place to somebody without telling us first. . . . However it is, the guy's got to learn he can't come into a place and start destroying gear first hop out of the box. And you know what the best way to learn is." He tossed a finished traphead into the box, and began a new one.

"Yes," said Lucy. "He finds his gear destroyed. So when do you cut his traps off?" She was careful to keep it expressionless, but he gave her a swift, slashing glance.

"I may just do that, come Monday morning."

If he expected her to protest that it wasn't the way they were brought up, she'd surprise him. *No* wasn't a word to slam at a Cameron.

"If I were you I'd just put it out of my mind till then," she said calmly.

"And maybe he'll disappear over the weekend, huh?" His laughter was cynical. "So I won't have to meet the problem head on. Or else he'll still be there and my traps still sunk, but I can say, Oh, forget it, there's lots worse that can happen."

She said angrily, "When I said that, we were talking about Penn. And lots worse *could* happen than his going to work instead of to college, and you know it! Anyway," she said more quietly, "I still think we should forget it all for a couple of days anyway and just think about something pleasant. Like going out tomorrow night. Are you and Donna going with us?"

"Nope." He pulled twine tight.

"Well, I don't care, as long as you're going out. All you think about is work and you deserve a little fun once in a while."

The telephone rang. "Scott!" She rushed happily to answer it.

"I'll go check on the boat." Geordie took the big flashlight from the shelf beside the clock and went out. Harold went too.

"This is Mrs. Morey." The voice was so crisp it fairly snapped in Lucy's ear. "Is Ralph there, by any chance?"

"Yes, he's here, Mrs. Morey. Didn't he call you?"

"No, he did not. Fortunately, someone has informed me that he left the school bus at your place."

Lucy's stomach twisted. "I'm sorry, Mrs. Morey," she said in her soft voice, "but I told Ralph to call you. I've been very busy around here and I thought he did. Would you like to speak to him? Or shall we bring him right in?"

"If you'll kindly tell him to wait by the mailbox, Mr. Morey will be straight out there to pick him up."

"I'll tell him, Mrs. Morey. And next time I'll be sure that he calls you up the first thing."

"There won't be a next time," said Mrs. Morey. "Good night."

"Good——" But the telephone at the other end had already been hung up.

Lucy's eyes blurred with tears and her throat clogged. She felt at once insulted and ashamed.

She couldn't call to Ralph while she felt like this. She

53

blew her nose hard, got her jacket from the hook, and went out the front door. Down at the shore Geordie's flashlight moved around the beached boat. She gazed up at Orion the hunter, with the blue-bright Dog Star Sirius straining ahead, until her eyes cleared and the cold purity of the night turned Mrs. Morey's actions into insignificance.

Then she went into the house again and found the singers run out of wind. The twins were feebly trying to wrestle each other into wakefulness, Ralph was reading, and Genie was saying brightly, "I know! I'll make us some cocoa!"

"No, you won't," said Lucy. "Ralph's mother called, and he's to be picked up at the mailbox right away."

Ralph sat up with his mouth open in horror. "I forgot!"

Genie looked as stricken as Ralph. "They must be some mad with you, Ralph, and probably with me too. They might not let you come out here again."

"Oh, don't talk so foolish," said Ralph, but it was a poor effort. So was his grin. "Well, I'd better get going."

"We'll walk up with you," suggested Philip.

"What, and get yourself waked up for the rest of the night?" asked Lucy. "No, *sir*. Go brush your teeth now, and get ready for bed."

Genie, having distractedly loaded Ralph with his books, was getting her jacket on. Ordinarily Lucy wouldn't have objected, but tonight was something different. If Mr. Morey came alone for Ralph, he might not

say anything. But if his wife was with him, and said anything to hurt Genie—— Lucy said sharply, "Genie, you
don't need to go."

Both Genie and Ralph looked at her in surprise; she
was never sharp. She said, "I mean it."

"But *why?*"

"Oh, for the love of Pete, Genie!" Ralph tried to
brush it off. "It's not like I'm scared of the dark!"

"That's not it." Genie wouldn't take her eyes off
Lucy. "I just want to go, and what's the harm?"

"What's the harm of what?" said Geordie from the
entry.

"Hi, Geordie," said Ralph with great relief. "I'm just
going. So long, everybody. Thanks for the swell supper, Luce. See you tomorrow, Genie." He shot out
past Geordie before Genie could protest. The back door
shut and he was gone.

Geordie lifted an eyebrow at the others. "What's this,
a branch of the waxworks? Or is everybody struck with
Spanish mildew?"

"Ask *her!*" cried Genie, and rushed from the room.
Lucy turned on the twins. "Why aren't you brushing
your teeth?" she demanded. They scampered for the
bathroom.

When they were all stowed away upstairs, Geordie
said, "What's going on?"

Lucy shrugged. "Oh, I'm tired tonight and I was a little sharp, I guess." She didn't want to tell him about
Mrs. Morey but, uneasy under those blue eyes, she had
to say something. "I knew Ralph wasn't all that crazy

about her walking up with him, in case his folks started bawling him out the first thing. He forgot to call his mother."

Geordie grinned. "Forgot on purpose, because she'd have told him to come straight home, most likely. Want some tea? Water's hot."

"I guess so. . . . Doesn't it make you mad, for the Moreys to act as if he'd get the plague here or something?"

"Nope. They had a right to get mad if he didn't call up. Makes no difference where he was. Besides, he's their only chick. Tough on him, of course," he added. He picked up his mug of tea and said, "I guess I'll watch *Gunsmoke*."

7

THERE WERE no lights in the house when Scott and Lucy drove into the yard late Saturday night. The headlights showed up the pickup in the barn. "Geordie's home and in bed already," Lucy said, "and he didn't leave till after we did—in fact, he hadn't even changed his clothes. I wonder where they went." She yawned, and snuggled deeper against Scott's shoulder. "Movies, most likely. . . . You know what? I feel almost like me again."

"You've felt like you to me all along," said Scott. "You sure smell like you." He put his nose against her hair and breathed deeply and said, "Ah-a-ah. Delicious."

She giggled. "Oh, you know what I mean. No, you don't, because you're not the oldest girl in a big family and you haven't suddenly become a parent . . . because that's what it amounts to." Her voice started to break, and Scott hugged her tighter.

"I'd take you out every night in the week, if it'd cheer you up," he said.

"See what I mean about being a parent? Instead of

saying, Oh, let's! the first thing I think of is getting to bed early because I have four kids to start off to school five mornings a week, and all those lunches."

Scott laughed. "Speaking of being a parent, you had a definite mother-look in your eye tonight when we walked into the Crow's Nest and saw Penn and Shelley."

"It was simply appraisal," she said with dignity. "She wasn't anything to me but the boss's daughter when I worked at the plant, but now she's Penn's girl. At least that's what Ralph says, and he's the fount of all information around here. . . . Let's talk about us, Scott." She turned her face into his neck. The discomfort she'd felt at coming face to face with Penn and Shelley hadn't been simply embarrassment at putting Penn on the spot. It was still with her, a definite unpleasantness she didn't want to examine too closely and thus take the luster off the evening.

They were having something to eat in the kitchen, while Harold gazed meltingly from one to the other, when Penn came in blinking at the light, wearing his clothes as if they'd been made for him, his clear skin warm brown against the white shirt. "Got some pie left?" he said.

"I shouldn't think you'd have room for pie after that steak you had in Limerock," said Lucy.

"Oh, that was just a snack for a growing boy," said Scott.

Penn laughed. "Too right." He poured milk and brought it to the table. "Well, Luce, what'd you think of her?"

"I don't think anything, for heaven's sake," said Lucy.

"She was polite, she smiled. We passed the time of day, and then Scott and I tactfully moved to the other end of the restaurant. So what was there to think about?"

"Well, what do you think of *me?*" Penn insisted. "Little brother dating the big man's daughter. Pretty good, huh?"

"Is Sears renting Westminster Abbey for the wedding?" asked Scott.

"He's toying with the thought," said Penn.

"*Are* you engaged, Penn?" Lucy heard herself asking the incredible question. "Is that why you won't try for college, and why you got the car, and everything?"

He had stopped laughing. His eyes, as blue and penetrating as Geordie's, met hers. She pushed on. "Why don't you bring her here for supper some night? Or would you be ashamed to?"

He pushed angrily back from the table. "No, I'm not ashamed! We've been hiding out from *her* folks, not mine, if you want to know! Her mother'd flip if she knew she was dating a lobsterman's son. But now I've got the car, and tonight we just thought, oh, the heck with it, let's be out in the open! We've got nothing to be ashamed of, either of us."

Scott reached out and touched his shoulder. "That's right. Good for you."

Penn said, "But I wouldn't bring her here and have Geordie look at us as if I was a fool and she was worse!"

Lucy made frantic signals to him to hush, and he leaned closer to the table and said in a low but savage voice, "Just because Geordie has bad luck with his women he doesn't want anybody else to have any fun.

Especially me. If I take my nose out of my books or out of the clam flats and make a date, I'm on my way to the devil."

"Listen, Geordie's got a lot on his mind," Scott said. "He worries about you kids."

"Kids," Penn sneered. "Who's a kid? I'm not. As for the younger ones, he's got a guilty conscience about them because he won't give them the breaks they could have."

Lucy heard it all but it was like the wind blowing past her ears. Only one phrase had stayed with her. "What do you mean about Geordie having bad luck with his women?"

"Didn't you know?" he said in honest astonishment. "Hey, Scott, didn't *you* know?"

The way Scott got up and refilled his cup told Lucy that he did know whatever it was, but that he'd kept it to himself.

"Didn't I know *what?*" she demanded coldly.

"Donna's broken off with Geordie. She's out tonight with the new guy. He's somebody in Limerock. I haven't found out who yet." He looked from one face to another. "Well, I tried to warn him how things looked —you remember, Luce, I kept saying things——"

"You kept sniping. Yes, I remember. Then he never went out at all tonight," she said to Scott in sick wonder. "He let me think he was going to get ready as soon as I cleared out, and all the time—oh, that *little*—oh, I could —who does she think she is, anyway?" Anger was rich and exhilarating. "I always did think she could be a two-timer, but I never thought she'd do it when Geordie had to stay away because his mother died! Well, I know *one* thing, she's not good enough for him and never was!"

"You're right about that," Penn agreed. "When she started to go out with him, it was when he was on the seining crew and making plenty. Now he's got to support a family. Everybody knows what she is. She'd go out with anybody who'd spend money on her." With a grin he added, "Even me. I could take her out in a minute."

"Penn, you wouldn't!"

"Of course I wouldn't," he said with dignity. "Geordie may be a real fire-and-brimstone type, but he's still my brother. Besides, I wouldn't go out with that little twerp on a bet. And twerp is the kindest word I could use about her. Boy, how he could have been so stupid!"

"She's pretty," said Lucy, defending Geordie's taste. "And she's fun when she wants to be. And she always looks so nice, she could be a model." Beneath Penn's cynical smile she ran out of conviction and said feebly, "She's smart, too. It takes brains to work in a bank."

"It's about money," said Penn. "That's why. She's bright enough when it's anything to do with cash."

"Well, anyway, there are lots of nice girls around who wouldn't mind going out with Geordie," said Lucy. "When we were in school, my gosh, the ones who were nice to me just because I was Geordie's sister!"

"Sam Cady told me about this girl who couldn't take her eyes off him," Scott said. "But he wouldn't give her a second look. It was down on the wharf yesterday. Good looking girl, too, Sam said."

"Girls could be buzzing around Geordie like bees and he'll still end up an old bach. And you two—" Penn paused and gave them a kindly look—"you better look out or you'll never get married, either."

"Gee, Gramp, thanks for the encouragement," said Scott. "Why don't you go to bed?"

"Just going, just going." When he'd gone upstairs, with Harold behind him on his way to rejoin the twins since nobody seemed to be doing any more eating, Lucy began nervously to clear the table and Scott helped her. She kept her face from him until he cornered her by the sink. "What's the matter?"

"What did he have to say *that* for?" she burst out in an angry whisper. "Oh, I know why. He thinks we should let the twins go to the Sylvesters, and Genie too. Imagine!"

"Yep, he's nuts to even suggest such a thing," said Scott. "But still——"

She froze, staring with anguish into his strong blunt face. "But still *what?*"

"We aren't going to wait till the kids are grown, are we?"

"Of course not! Genie's growing up fast, you know, and she's real capable around the house. The twins can do a lot, too. Might be I could leave her in charge in a year or so, as long as I was in town here and could advise her, and look after any of them if they were sick."

The more she said, the better it sounded. She began to feel happier—guiltily so, because of Geordie's bad luck. Scott pulled her into his arms and rocked her back and forth. "Look, even if I'm in the service when the year's up, we'll get married anyway. First leave I can get. How's that?"

"It sounds so wonderful it makes me sick," said Lucy. "A nice sick, though. It's just that a year's so long."

He kissed her and said, "If they draft me why couldn't we get married anyway, before I get sent anywhere? That way you'd still be here with the kids, but whenever I get a chance to come home we could get off and stay by ourselves for that time."

She couldn't answer this, but found herself on the edge of tears.

"What are you sniffling about?" he whispered.

"Because I'm happy. But I still don't want you to be drafted. Oh, I don't know *what* I want!"

"You do too know. You want me." They ended up laughing, delightfully foolish without having any reason for it, and then she went out to the car with him to say good night.

8

G EORDIE WOKE Monday morning with a sense of deep oppression. Something bad had happened and something else was going to happen that he'd like to avoid. The moment he opened his eyes in the chilly dark he remembered both things. One was Donna, and the weekend hadn't made the ache any the less. The other concerned the squatter and the lost gear. He groaned. Time was when he could hardly wait to get out of bed in the morning. And here he was, not yet twenty-one, pitching into sleep at night like an alcoholic into his bottle, and waking in the morning as if he had all the sins of eighty years on his conscience.

He dressed and went downstairs, not sure of anything except that Life was terrible. Marm was fond of quoting something out of some book she'd always liked: "It isn't life that matters, but the courage that you bring to it."

Well, she'd known all about courage, she and the old man both. Too bad they hadn't been able to live and keep dosing their kids with it.

Harold had come downstairs behind him. Geordie let him out and took a deep breath of the cold air. Then he heard a faint sound like dogs barking very far off, and he stepped outside to listen. Nearer and nearer it came, but always high overhead, and though it was dark yet, he stared upward as if he could see the sound when it passed over.

The voices of the wild Canada geese flying south. . . . He knew how the long V looked trailing across the sky, wavering yet firm. Even as a child he had wondered about the leader at the very apex of the V with the two lines streaming back from him. How was he chosen? Was he the oldest, the wisest, the one who had made the trip so many times he carried in his brain a chart of the best ways over ocean, woods, farmland, cities? The one who knew the safest places to rest and feed, where no hunters came? Sometimes as Geordie watched with straining eyes, not wanting to miss a sight or sound of them, he'd seen another one move up and take the leader's place. How was *that* decided?

And all the time they cried back and forth to one another, in constant communication. What were they saying? Nobody knew. It had been one of his first disappointments, that his father didn't know.

Wryly he admitted now that he wouldn't know either what to tell the twins if they asked him. Not that they were likely to. As far as he knew, he was the only one who felt the leap in his chest like joy when he heard them coming north in the spring, and knew this sadness in the fall.

Because of thinking and wondering so much about the geese, he couldn't hunt them. How many of them would make it south, how many of these same birds would fly over Cameron Cove on their way to their northern sanctuaries? . . . Harold came running back and jumped up on him with frost-wet feet. They went back into the warm kitchen and Geordie began to get his breakfast.

Lucy'd be up soon enough to get the kids started but he didn't want to talk to her this morning. She'd be trying not to show how sorry she was for him, making out she didn't know anything about him and Donna, and that would be just plain awful.

He began to hurry, not stopping to eat, filling his thermos with coffee and the jug with water, hacking off slices of cold pot roast and making thick sandwiches for his lunchbox. He got a couple of apples from the cold entry, put in some doughnuts and a handful of molasses cookies, and left the house just as the first creaks and thumps sounded from upstairs.

The eastern sky was the warm color of ripe peaches and the water reflected it. His rubber boots made black tracks in the silver bloom of frost. The air was so still he could hear engines warming up over at the harbor.

Walking down the wharf, he envied the old gander's wisdom. If only he could have a bit of it to keep *his* flock and himself in a straight line. . . . He took oilskins and lunchbox and water jug down the ladder and into the skiff. *Mary C.* rode the high tide at her mooring, her name and home port glistened in black across her stern, her registration numbers as sharp on either side of her bow. Beneath them, also on either side, there was the painting of a lobster buoy in the Cameron colors, blue and yellow. This was the new law. Genie'd done the buoys and Penn the lettering, Sunday morning after the white paint dried. Penn had offered; that was the big surprise. It was as if he couldn't understand Geordie's not hitting the roof about the car, and it made him uneasy. Unless, Geordie reflected sardonically, Penn was actually *sorry* for him. . . . Sure, he'd heard Penn telling Lucy and Scott about Donna that night; he hadn't been able to get to sleep, and thought he'd go down to the kitchen with the others, and when he was halfway down the stairs he'd heard Penn say, "Didn't you know? Hey, Scott, didn't *you* know?"

Penn's description of Donna had sent him back to bed to lie wounded and furious in the dark. He suspected it was the truth, and he didn't want it to be. He'd rather think she'd fallen for some guy so hard she couldn't help herself—even though the thought made him writhe— than know she walked out because he didn't have the money to spend on her anymore.

As he headed out of the harbor the ripe peach tint was fading into the palest of blues. The Nuggets lay to the south. With their tawny rocks and their grass turned yellow-brown, and the sun striking them just right, they really looked like rough chunks of gold.

The first blue-and-yellow buoy showed ahead. Geordie slowed down, his gaff ready.

You could clean him out in one night, he told himself. He couldn't prove anything to the warden any more than I could. But he'd get the message and move off. We don't need any of his kind around here. . . . Sure, Pa didn't bring you up to think like that. But had he ever run into anything like this when he had to make every penny count? No, you didn't, Pa, Geordie answered

67

himself. And if you had, I bet that old Highland blood would have boiled, and you could have used a knife with the best of 'em.

So that was it, wasn't it? Couldn't have been plainer. That's what Pa would have done. *No, it wasn't*. And his son was already turning the wheel hard over, heading directly for the Nuggets. With a sigh that seemed to come up from his boots Geordie pondered the questions. Was he his own man? Was he a man at all, in fact, if he couldn't go against what Pa would have done? Or was this some of the old gander's wisdom that he'd wished for this morning? And if the squatter met him with a shotgun blast when he showed his face up over the wharf, he might have just time enough left to realize it was all tomfoolery.

He went full speed for the Nuggets; *Mary C.* seemed to fly across liquid glass that shattered her bow into flashing splinters. As he approached a spatter of buoys that showed scarred red-and-white stripes he slowed down, and went cautiously through them. The man hadn't wasted any time throwing his pots overboard. He'd probably hauled them twice already.

As he entered the channel between Gold and Copper, he saw the boat tied up at the rickety wharf. A thin girl in slacks stood on the wharf, hanging on to two young children by the hands. The man was down aboard the boat. He knew they'd all seen him. Even the kids stopped wriggling and were looking. It was sort of unnerving, this silent staring. His face grew red, and he kept busy looking over the side as he edged up to the wharf.

68

Then he shut off the engine and held himself off from the gypsy boat by his gaff. He looked up at the girl and touched his cap. " 'Morning," he said gruffly. She didn't answer. Her eyes seemed to half-fill her face, and close to she didn't look much older than Genie. The kids were big-eyed, puny, and silent too. The man in the boat was young, a lot shorter than Geordie, skinny, with sharp features. He looked at Geordie through hostile slits in a sunburned, hatchet-jawed face.

"You want something?" It would have been a growl if his voice had been deep enough. The hand holding a wrench twitched. Instantly Geordie felt a lot calmer himself, as if he were in charge of the situation.

"Just introducing myself," he said, sitting down on the engine box. "I'm Geordie Cameron. If you happened to look at the names on those buoys you cut off, you'd have seen it was mine."

"You can't prove anything!" the girl cried at once.

"You hush up, Weezie," the man said without looking away from Geordie. "You take the kids and go up to the house."

"Yes, but Mike———"

"You *git*."

"Mike Tolman, you be careful!" She turned, her face twisted with anxiety, and as she and the children trailed up the wharf, the black cat came out from among the traps and followed them.

"Now, *Mister* Cameron," said the man in a tight, jerky voice. "Where's your gun?"

"Gun?" Geordie was startled. "What are you looking for, a duel? I don't carry any guns aboard here."

69

"You figger you're going to take me to pieces with your fists then, is that it?" He dropped the wrench and showed his own fists. "Come ahead!"

Geordie wanted to laugh. All he could think of was the bantam rooster they'd had for years, who always wanted to take on everything and everybody that came into the dooryard. "Listen, I didn't come to shoot you, or beat you up. I just want to know what right you've got to cut off my traps. I know I didn't see you do it, but you're the only one who could've, or who'd want to."

"I ain't saying whether I did or I didn't. But if I did—and mind you I ain't saying I did—I had a right to warn you guys off in the only language you'd understand. Because *I'm* living here now, see? Maybe you think you've fished it so long you've got some kind of rights yourself, but *I'm* the one with rights." He would have kept on but Geordie interrupted him and talked him down, coldly and calmly.

"Maybe before you run out of wind you'll tell me just what those rights are. And before that, what do you mean about the only language we'd understand? You don't know us from Hannah Cook. You don't know what we understand and don't understand. I'll tell you one thing, little man. Around here, no matter what a man claims his rights are, he just doesn't walk in and start destroying property without an aye, yes, or no." At the words "little man" Mike's face became scarlet, and he hauled in a big breath.

"Well, now mebbe you'll make no mistake about the kind of man *I* am!" he exploded. "Maybe *that's* why I did it!"

"Oh, so you did it."

"*If* I did it, that's why!"

Geordie wanted to laugh again. The Lord knew he had nothing to laugh about, but he wanted to, just the same.

"Is all that blowing and sputtering and dancing meant to convey the fact that you got some sort of legal position here?"

"Ayuh, I got legal rights! My father owns this bunch of islands! That plain enough for ye?"

By an effort Geordie continued to look in charge of the situation. "Does that make Burt Watson some relation of yours? Uncle or cousin or something? Did he know you were moving in?"

"He's something, I'd say. But I'd hate to say what. And why in Tophet should he know what *I* do? I never laid eyes on the gink and hope I never do."

"Well, you most likely will as soon as he gets home from Boston," said Geordie, "because he owns the Nuggets too. Your father must be that half-brother or whatever, who went out West."

"Grandfather," said Mike. "Walked out on his wife and boy, the old buzzard. Died ten years ago, good riddance to bad rubbish, and my father got this place. Now he's dead and it's mine."

"Half of it," said Geordie. "Where'd you come from?"

Mike squinted ferociously. "You gonna have me investigated? Well, you won't find nothing bad. I warn't run out of town."

"For Pete's sake, can't anybody ask a simple question?" said Geordie in disgust. "You come from the east'ard, or the west'ard?"

"East'ard. You satisfied? I been in and gassed up this morning, and the warden, *he* went over me with a fine-tooth comb. He knows where I come from now, he's satisfied I'm who I say I am. So I don't need it from you."

"You tell him how you get your messages across?" asked Geordie, "or shall we?"

Mike flinched, and Geordie guessed at the doubts and fears that gripped him. He was in a strange place, legally or not, and Geordie might be a good friend of the warden. He moved in quickly. "I'll tell you something," Geordie said. "I've been considering how to get *my* message across."

"Is this a warning?" Mike was grayish under his sunburn, but his eyes never shifted.

"You can take it that way. Listen, why in time didn't you wait till you saw me coming out here to haul, and then come alongside and tell me who you were?"

"Would you've shifted your gear?"

"I don't have to. A man with a license can set his traps anywhere. But there's plenty of room for two fishermen here."

"Not as I see it," Mike sneered. "You fellers only understand one kind of language and I can talk it as good as anybody."

Geordie sighed. "You don't know us fellers from a hole in the ground, so don't start telling us what we're like. Okay. You say you've got a right to be fishing here, and if that's the truth, nobody'll bother you. But it would have given you a darn sight better start if you hadn't cost me over a hundred dollars in gear."

He sat down on the engine box. "Well, I'm not about to beat you up, though you're asking for it, and I'm not about to smash up any of your gear, though from the looks of it all the traps you've got wouldn't make up for the ones I lost. But I'll tell you this. Because of the way you made yourself known when you moved in, I'll be just waiting for you to step out of line. Behave yourself, and you'll be all right. Otherwise——" He slashed his fingers across his throat. "Understand?"

Mike's eyes were animal-bright, his mouth a tight pale line. He didn't speak or even nod, just stared.

"And don't try living on short lobsters either," Geordie said. "That doesn't go around here." He started his engine and backed the boat away from the wharf. He glanced up toward the camp and ironically waved to the girl. She didn't move, but one of the children timidly waved back. At the wharf, Mike was still motionless.

Geordie felt neither relief nor triumph. He worked the rest of the day like a hauling machine shaped like a man. He didn't even think of Mike Tolman again and the big-eyed girl and the children. He didn't decide whether to set more traps back there or not. It was all Donna, as if shock had numbed him over the weekend but now he was fully awake to the pain. Longing and fury shook him in alternate waves; he wanted to shake her until she cried, to hug her till her ribs cracked, and most of all he wanted to crash his big fist into the unknown man's face.

When he found himself on the way to the harbor with his day's work behind him, it was like waking from a dream. He was shaking out the old bait from the bags and the gulls were following him in a screaming, flapping cloud, with sunset on their wings. His crates were full, and he could hardly remember plugging the lobsters that went into them. He felt physically exhausted and yet his body kept going through the proper motions, like a well-maintained machine.

There were other boats ahead of him at the lobster car, and he shut his engine off and waited his turn, looking down past the moorings toward the Blake house. She's gone, he thought. She's really gone. And he was too tired to do anything but know it was the truth.

$\sim\sim\sim\sim\sim\sim\sim\sim\sim\sim\sim\sim\sim\sim\sim\sim\sim\sim\sim\sim$

I T WOULD be the first Christmas without their parents. Lucy wished there were a way to go far out around it and take up life again in January. But the twins had been getting ready for Christmas since Thanksgiving. They were making things in school to decorate the windows, they were practicing for the Christmas pageant in Sunday school, they sang *Jingle Bells* and carols all over the place. They'd wanted to go looking for a tree on the first of December. Television and the mail-order catalogues told them constantly that they wanted all kinds of magical, marvelous things.

Which, of course, they wouldn't get. Lobstering hadn't been terrible, but it hadn't been very good, either, and there'd be more wind and bad weather as the winter deepened, not less. But the children would be pleased with whatever they got. All the Camerons had been brought up to cherish the atmosphere of Christmas: getting and trimming the tree, singing carols, loving the story of Bethlehem and the star. If the shine had gone out of it for Lucy this year, she'd try to keep the younger ones from knowing it.

The first good snowfall came on a Friday night, and on the sunny Saturday morning the twins went out to coast in the old pasture, accompanied by Harold. Geordie had gone to haul, Penn to his Christmas job in Limerock, and Genie sat opposite Lucy at the kitchen table while Lucy tried to make out a list.

She scribbled, crossed out, talked to herself and to Genie. "Scott's sister is going to let me have those skates for a dollar, and if I can find another secondhand pair, you could give the twins a puck, and Geordie could give them hockey sticks, and——"

The silence from across the table finally penetrated her busy mind. She looked up. Genie's dark eyes moved toward her, and they were anguished. "Oh, honey," Lucy said impulsively, "I *know*. But we can't cheat the little kids."

"It's not that," said Genie in a funny, cracked little voice. "I mean it *is,* kind of. I try not to remember last Christmas. But what makes it even worse is——" She stared across the room at the telephone. "It's almost ten o'clock and Ralph hasn't called up! He didn't call up last night either. That makes two Saturdays we haven't done anything, and—oh, Luce!" she burst out. "He's acting so *funny!* He's not like Ralph at all! He doesn't even come near me in the bus!" She jumped up. "It's because you wouldn't let me walk up the lane with him that night. I'll bet he thinks you and Geordie don't want me to be with him anymore. And he was my best friend, my *absolutely best* friend!"

She ran noisily up the stairs and to her room. Lucy tried to look at her list but she couldn't think of it anymore. She thought instead of Scott, and she longed for him so much that her throat hurt and she wanted to call him up this instant and hear his voice. Then she felt guilty because she still had Scott while Geordie'd lost Donna, and Genie her "absolutely best friend."

She went up and knocked on Genie's door. Genie didn't answer, but Lucy could hear her sobbing, so she knocked louder. Genie became silent, and still didn't answer.

"I want to tell you something," Lucy said. "I tried to save your feelings, but they've been hurt anyway, and I'm tired of taking the blame for it."

Genie opened the door and stared defiantly at her from puffy eyes. "Well?"

"I wouldn't let you walk up with him that night because if his mother drove out with Mr. Morey to get him she might have said something real nasty to you, she was so mad with Ralph. That's all. And I think Ralph was worried about that too, so he was probably relieved when I wouldn't let you go."

"Why didn't you tell me then? That night?"

Lucy shrugged helplessly. "I'm new at this, Genie. Being a mother, I mean."

Genie's mouth trembled in an uncertain smile. "Specially to a daughter only four years younger than you are. . . . Well, I guess I—I can see how it was. . . . They must have told Ralph to stay away from me——" She was still trying hard for valor. "Maybe they think I'm a d-dangerous influence, and I'll lead Ralph astray!" Her giggle hiccuped into an angry sob. Her cheeks were flaming red. "But *I'd* never turn *my* back on my best friend, no matter what! If that's the way Ralph is, I'm glad I found out! Now I can stop thinking about it and get on with my life!"

Her face twisted up and she turned blindly away. Lucy went out and shut the door.

She'll live, she thought. Maybe it's better happening now, so she can get it over with. But she was trembling herself, and she couldn't concentrate on her Christmas list now.

She kicked off her loafers and put on her boots, pulled on the dark red turtleneck sweater her mother had knit for her last Christmas, one of Geordie's wool shirts over it, and went out. There was no wind and the sun was warm. The shadows of the house and of the spruce trees were as blue on the snow as forget-me-nots. The sea picked up the color and carried it to the horizon. The heat of the sun struck a spicy fragrance from the thick banking of fresh spruce boughs packed around the foundation of the house. From beyond the trees on the rise came the children's cries and Harold's barking. She turned toward the path that led up the rocky hill beyond the barn. Maybe if she watched the kids coast for a while she'd get things back into focus. . . . Was this how mothers felt when one of their children was suffering and they couldn't help?

"Hey, Luce!" A piercing whistle followed the cry. She swung around. A familiar stocky figure was slogging along through the melting snow and mud of the lane. Even from this distance she could see his grin.

Ralph. She went slowly back and waited by the open barn doors. When he came up to her he said, "I woke up this morning and I knew it would be a good day to get the Christmas tree. . . . You haven't got it yet, have you?" He sounded alarmed.

"Ralph, does your mother know you're out here?"

Keeping his eyes on hers, he said, "Yes. Genie coasting with the kids?"

"No," Lucy said. "Why don't you go on over, and Genie and I'll come along and bring the ax, and something to eat."

"All right!" He started cheerfully up the path and Lucy went back to the house. Would a real mother know if Ralph was lying or not? Should she have asked him straight out? But he'd looked her right in the eye. Mrs. Morey had probably gotten over her anger and lifted her restrictions. Yes, that was the way it was. She was sure of it.

She went into the house shouting, "Genie! Come on down, help me get a lunch together!"

The Sylvesters were loyal to the children they wanted. The mail driver began leaving notes in the mailbox about parcels too big to put in the box; they had to be picked up in town at the post office. Penn brought back the first batch, one carton addressed to the Cameron family, the other to the twins.

"They never give up, do they?" he said.

"It's perfectly natural for them to send things," Lucy protested. "Uncle Bill was Marm's only brother. They've always sent things."

"But not this much. This is all just to show the twins what it's like up there in the Promised Land."

"Oh, don't be so cynical." Lucy tried to sound amused, but she was uneasy about Geordie, who was knitting trapheads without looking around. "And put those boxes up under Geordie's bed, before the kids come in, will you?"

When he'd gone upstairs, singing loudly, *Deck the Halls,* Geordie said, "You have any second thoughts about hanging on to the twins?"

"No!" She was shocked. "Do you?"

"No. But they might get some ideas of their own. Penn's right, much as I hate to admit it. . . . . What we've got for them will look pretty sick beside the baseball gear and the trains, not to mention the new clothes."

"They don't know anything about these things," she said steadily. "We don't have to let them have them."

"For Pete's sake, I *want* them to have all that stuff! I'd just like to be the one to give it, that's all. And where they want the kids, it makes it all that harder to accept it."

"As if we shouldn't take anything if we're not willing to let the kids go," she said. He nodded with a savage jerk of his long jaw, and pulled the twine so tight it sang.

"Well," said Lucy, "I'm sure the kids wouldn't want to leave us, no matter what. And we never *asked* the Sylvesters to send them presents. So I don't see why they can't accept. They can write nice thank-you notes, and we'll let it go at that."

"You make it sound so simple," said Geordie grimly.

"Hey, Luce!" Penn called down the stairs. "One of these boxes won't go under Geordie's bed. Where'd you want to put it?"

She ran up the stairs and met him in the hall. "Have you got room in your closet, or is it too full of your clothes?"

"Cripes," Penn muttered. "I thought I was doing well by the kids, but our rich relatives are putting us all in the shade."

"Honestly, the way you and Geordie take on. . . ! They'll love whatever you give them, and I'll love whatever you give me." She grinned at him. "That is, if you're giving me a Christmas present. Maybe you aren't."

"Wait till you see it! It's something you've always wanted."

"Let's see, that gives me a choice of about a million things. It's not a brand-new all-electric kitchen, is it? Or my own bathroom all in black tile with a sunken tub?"

"That's it! How'd you guess?" They both laughed. Like Geordie he was completely transformed by laughter, only in Geordie's case the transformation came too seldom these days. "Hey, want to see what I've got for Genie?" He dragged a box out from the depths of his closet, and put it on his bed. He opened it and lifted out a small portable record player. "Look at that! Runs on six flashlight batteries, and plays four speeds. She can take it outdoors, anywhere."

"She'll flip, Penn, she really will. I see where from now on all Genie's presents are records."

"I've already got her a couple of albums." He dug those out from under his shirts. "She's crazy about The Lost Chords. Shelley picked out the other one. She says all girls are romantic at heart even if they don't admit it. *Music to Dream By,*" he read. "I said Genie's never quiet enough to dream except when she's asleep, but she said 'Don't you believe it, she gets plenty of dreaming in.' "

"Shelley sounds nice," Lucy said shyly.

"She is." He turned away quickly and began putting the record albums under his shirts again. "Want to see what I'm giving her?" he asked.

"I'd love to," she said. She felt a curious excitement, not exactly pleasant; but it was familiar, it had always rested like a cloud around Shelley's name from the first time she'd heard it linked with Penn's. He had a small box in his hand, and she recognized the name of the jeweler's shop in Limerock. He took off the lid and she saw, embedded in white velvet, a pendant of rich dark-red stones and gold filigree as fine as lace. "It's beautiful," she murmured. "I never saw anything so beautiful. It looks very old."

"She likes things like that," he said in an offhand manner. "She's funny that way."

"I like her more and more," said Lucy, trying to make a joke out of it. "Penn, why don't you bring her over some night during the holidays? We could get Scott, and Craig and Linda, and they could bring a girl for Geordie."

Penn's face went stony. "Go ahead," he said. "But not with Shelley and me, Luce. She wouldn't go for that. She just wouldn't fit, she's too sophisticated. Besides, what makes you think Geordie'd soften up all at once and be the life of the party? Specter at the Feast would be more like it. There's times when I don't blame Donna."

He began busily packing up the record player again, and put it away without looking at her once. She wanted to hit him, an impulse which was foreign to her.

"You're spending too much money," she said. "The car, and new clothes, and now all these expensive presents. You'll have nothing left pretty soon."

"What's it to you? I earned it myself. I pay my board, don't I? And half the telephone bill? Pay Genie for doing my shirts and tending my room?"

"The star boarder," she said. "That's what you are, and *all* you are." She wanted to stop, but she couldn't. The hurt in her made her want to hurt him. "You're not our brother. You wouldn't put yourself out one inch for the rest of us, even at Christmas."

"Hey, what's eating you?" He was genuinely astonished. "Luce, you're all shook up these days. You don't act any more like yourself than——" He spread out his hands to show that he was beyond words. "I know what the trouble is. You want to get married, and all you can see ahead is raising the kids and keeping house for Geordie. I'm sorry for you, Luce, I really am." He shook his head and looked properly sorrowful. "And the heck of it is that you don't *have* to live that way."

She drew in a long breath of outrage, stared into his earnest blue eyes, and then walked out of the room. The horror of the moment was that, if she'd allow herself to face the truth, Penn was at least half right.

Geordie had gone out. Ignoring her own rule about calling Scott at the lobster-shipping plant, she went straight to the telephone and dialed the number.

"Barstow & Cady," a girl's voice answered. "Good morning!"

"Hi, Linda," Lucy tried to sound casual. Linda went with Craig, Scott's brother. "Is Scott busy? If he's packing, don't call him, but if he's just having a coffee break——"

"The two of them are having one," said Linda, "and cluttering up the premises and interfering with my work. Scott, it's for you.   —Lucy, somebody was asking me all kinds of questions about Geordie the other day. She's —oh, all *right*, Scott!" Hastily she added, "If I ever get a chance I'll tell you all about her, Lucy. So long!"

Scott came on, blessedly calm. "Anything wrong?" His voice made her feel very safe, and she was ashamed now of her cowardice. "I just felt like saying hello," she said.

"Hello," he said. They both laughed.

"I must have been psychic, catching you in the office."

"I'm glad you did. Or were. Whichever it is."

"So am I. Isn't this a silly conversation?" Geordie was coming back in. "So long, Scott."

"See you tonight," he said. She hung up with a wonderful sense that everything was all right again—or as right as it could be at Christmas without Marm and Pa. . . . And Penn was *wrong*.

10

P ENN managed to miss the Sunday-school pageant, but he did spend Christmas Eve with them and sang carols as loud as anybody; and he spent all of Christmas Day, not going off to town until after supper that night. Lucy wondered skeptically if it was because Shelley was expected to devote that much time exclusively to her family. Or was she doing Penn an injustice? He'd loved his parents, and Christmas had always been a good time in the old Cameron house, even without much money to spend. It meant fir-tree branches and spicy baking, tangerines in the tips of the stockings, homemade wreaths decorated with gilded nuts and seed pods; mysterious whisperings; the reverent delight of assembling the manger scene on the mantel above the Franklin stove in the living room, and the separate delight in stringing cranberries and popcorn for the tree, and making endless paper chains and everything else scissors and paste could devise. It meant the shimmer of the old ornaments as they were carefully unwrapped. This year it meant Geordie putting the angel on top of the tall tree, because their father had always done so, with Penn being the electrician and testing the lights. It meant bows and bells on Harold's collar, and a special beef bone, gift-wrapped and kept in the refrigerator till Christmas morning, because otherwise he'd dig his way through the pile of things under the tree to locate it.

The relatives had included things for the whole family, but they'd gone all out on the younger ones.

"Wow!" Philip breathed. "Uncle Bill must be some *rich!*" He slapped a baseball (autographed by Yastrzemski) into a catcher's mitt.

"He isn't rich," Genie said. "He's just got a good job and no kids, that's all."

"But he and Aunt Nora wish they had kids like us," said Peter, fondling a locomotive. "She said so."

"If they do, it's because distance lends enchantment to the view," Genie told him. "Don't be so stuck on yourself."

"I'd like to go and live with 'em," Philip said, and the words stabbed Lucy through. "Long enough to see the Red Sox play. Hey, when can we go skating?"

"Yeah, we been wanting skates all our life," said Peter solemnly, picking his up. "And now we got 'em."

Lucy and Genie swapped relieved grins over the two red heads. Secondhand skates meant just as much to the boys as the new and dazzling things from the outside world.

Lucy had clung to her idea of a party, and she began thinking of it for New Year's Eve. She didn't want to go heartlessly off with Scott, leaving Geordie to brood about Donna. She made a list of people they could invite, and planned a midnight feast around her own incomparable baked beans. But when she mentioned it to Geordie, the afternoon after Christmas when the others had all gone skating at the village, he shook his head.

"You go on out with Scott."

"But I don't want to leave you!" she objected.

"Look, you worry about the little kids. Or about yourself. I'll worry about *me*." He tapped himself on the chest. "I'd a darn sight rather kick around here and not have to worry about my manners than make small talk with some nitwit pal of Linda's."

"How do you know she'd be a nitwit?"

"Because Linda's one. And because any girl that's left unattached on New Year's Eve must have a heck of a lot wrong with her."

"Or else she's choosy! Maybe she's never seen anybody to suit her up to now. You men always assume that if a girl doesn't have a date it's because nobody's asked her. Well, she just *might* be turning them all down because she's particular."

Geordie's eyes glinted. "Seems to me you're getting all worked up about a girl who doesn't even exist."

"How do you know she doesn't exist, Geordie Cameron?" Lucy demanded. "Remember a girl down on the wharf once when you came in? Well, she's moving into town and she asked Linda who you were, and *she's* not a nitwit."

"How can Linda tell?" he teased her. "Ayuh. I remember. She was with a boy friend old enough to be her father."

"He *is* her father," she said smugly. "He's an artist, and they're buying the old Davis place on the harbor. She goes to the University of Maine."

"Sounds perfect for me," said Geordie. "No, thanks. Women are the last thing I'm interested in these days."

"I could shake you!" she exploded. "You don't think there's another girl in the world besides Donna. Talk about nitwits! Nasty two-faced little nitwits who can't even do their own dirty work!"

Geordie looked calmly at her. "Pipe down before you blow a gasket, Luce. I know you mean well, but Donna didn't commit a crime when she called it off, and it might be she has plenty on her side. As far as not telling me herself, well, she knew it had to be done, but she was too soft-hearted to face me."

"She's about as soft-hearted as one of those granite ledges sticking out of the hill. Why, Harold's more of a *good person* than she is!"

"Mebbe so," said Geordie with annoying stolidity. "And I'd rather stick around here exchanging views with Harold on New Year's Eve than with some girl you've dragged in out of pity."

"Well, thank you very much, Cap'n Cameron," said Lucy, tight-lipped. She pulled on her boots and went out to take in the wash.

In a few minutes Geordie came out the back door with Harold, and she expected him to go back to the fishhouse without speaking to her. Instead, he came out to the clotheslines and stood looking around, his hands in his pockets. "Feels like March out here," he said finally. "I wish it was."

"So do I. Can't we just forget New Year's?"

"I already have." He grinned at her and went back down to the fishhouse. She looked sadly after him. That girl *did* exist! But who could find her if Geordie wouldn't?

As the dusk set in, Geordie drove in to town to pick up the skaters, and Lucy began to get supper. In a little while the truck was back, and a torrent of human and canine sounds flowed into the kitchen as if a dam had burst. The twins were both talking at once and Genie was trying to exercise her seniority and talk above them, while Harold outdid them all. Only Geordie was silent, setting his boots behind the stove and going into the other room without even a glance at Lucy.

Now what? Maybe he'd seen Donna at the pond with somebody. . . . She turned in response to Peter's tug on her arm. "Guess what! Penn and Shelley bought us hot dogs!"

"I had a hamburger!" Philip yelled. "Peter ate three hot dogs!" Peter punched him and said, "Let *me* tell it. We had Cokes, too."

"Oh?" said Lucy. She looked across at Genie. "Does Geordie know?"

"Oh, sure. *They* told him right away. Well, why shouldn't he know, Luce?" she argued. "She's Penn's girl, and they're out in the open now. He's even been to her house. He drives her to school every day since he got the car. . . . She's teaching me figure skating." She waltzed dreamily around the kitchen, eyes glazed, and hummed the *Skater's Waltz*. As she glided past Lucy she said very softly, "Luce, they're in *love*."

Scott called up shortly, very hoarse with a sore throat, to say he wouldn't be over that night. Lucy went to bed very early that night with an apple and a library book. Genie and Geordie were watching a movie downstairs, and Lucy settled down in guilty comfort. She knew she was only postponing the moment when Geordie would put into words her belief that Penn was taking a cheap and easy path by playing up to a rich man's daughter. She didn't for a moment believe that he was in love with this shy girl. But he could play the part well, always looking out for Penn, and use Shelley as a steppingstone to a well-paying job where he'd have a lot more money to spend on cars and clothes and girls.

This was the source of the queasiness that afflicted Lucy whenever she thought of Shelley and Penn together. It had been strong the night in the Crow's Nest when she had seen the way Shelley was looking at Penn while he was looking elsewhere. She was in love, all right, or thought she was. But Penn?

Geordie didn't bring the subject up the next day or the next. New Year's passed, and the children went back to school. Now the older ones missed their parents the most; Geordie working alone in the fishhouse through the freezing, windy days with only the snapping fire for company, Lucy up in the house. But the days were moving faster now, hurrying through January, whereas last October each day had endured for a year.

Lucy went out with Scott whenever they had good weather on a Friday or Saturday night, and Geordie didn't go out with anyone. She'd have been happier if he'd at least driven to town and played cards with the other Volunteer Firemen on Friday nights, or had stood around the wharves for an hour now and then, talking with the other men. Yet she didn't know what to say to him, and then she'd reason that he was well rid of Donna, and someone just right would come along sooner or later. . . .

"But she'll have to find her way to Cameron Point by ESP and grab him," she told Scott. "He's not taking any chances on being ambushed away from home. What about that new girl?"

"Christy? She's back at college."

"No, I mean what's she *like?*"

He shrugged. "I don't know her. She's been out with Mont Cady, and Craig and Linda, they like her, she plays a guitar. That's all I can tell you."

"She might have taken Geordie's mind up for a while," Lucy brooded. "Now she's probably lost interest."

"What are you so worried about?" Scott asked.

"He should have a girl! He's almost twenty-one!"

"Practically senile," Scott teased her. "Leave him alone. Come spring and he'll likely blossom like a daffodil."

"You mean he'll turn into a flower child?"

The idea was so funny that she had to laugh, and for a while after that she didn't worry so much about Geordie.

They had all written thanks to the Sylvesters for their gifts. Now the Sylvesters wrote inviting the twins to spend the February vacation with them.

"No!" Geordie exploded. Lucy agreed, resenting

the invitation as a threat to their hard-earned security. Fortunately the children didn't know of it, and neither she nor Geordie intended that they should know. Death had reached into their home and stolen their father and mother; now something else was trying to steal the children. What if one came home from these visits wanting to go live with Uncle Bill and Aunt Nora?

I'd die, Lucy thought in the middle of the night. I'd just die. . . . She got out of bed and went down the hall to the twins' room. Harold sprawled across the foot of the big double bed, thumping his tail softly against the footboard, and she fondled his ears while she studied the twins in the indirect glow of her flashlight.

On her way back to her room, she met Geordie. "They all right?" he whispered.

"Yes. Why?"

"I had the darndest dream about them. It got me up."

"Let's go down and get something to eat."

As if the whispered word *eat* had reached him around several corners, Harold joined them. Lucy brooded over a mug of tea while Geordie and Harold shared crackers and rat-trap cheese. The dream shaken off—a dream of waking up to find the twins mysteriously stolen from their beds on this winter's night—Geordie was almost lightheaded with relief, and very hungry. But when he looked across at Lucy he saw the shadows under her eyes and a sadness that seemed too deep for tears.

"Look, Luce," he said, "they can't just walk in and take the kids, you know. So cheer up. Or is it something else? The draft? Or are you afraid he'll lose interest like——" He stopped abruptly.

"No, it's not Scott this time," she said. "But there's always something. Take your pick. What if Penn's right and we're cheating the kids, and someday they hold it against us?"

"They'd be more likely to hold it against us someday if we gave them away now."

"Then why are we afraid to let them go spend four or five days with relatives? Other people do it, and they aren't scared."

"We can't go by what other people do. Just by what we know." He wagged a saltine at her. "Now I don't think Uncle Bill and his wife are a couple of reprobates for being crazy about our kids. They've got none of their own and ours look pretty special to them. Right?" She nodded bleakly. "And they figger we want to get married and live our own lives, so we just *might* weaken. So they're going to woo those kids like mad, with everything they've got. Now, write to 'em tomorrow, tell 'em the kids can't go, and put the whole thing out of your mind."

"There's April vacation. There's next summer. Ten weeks of it. They'll keep after us."

He grinned at her. "Worry Wart. *Don't* write tomorrow, then. Don't forget, next week I'll be twenty-one, and Mr. Bartlett's going with me to see his lawyer in Limerock about drawing up the guardianship petition. I've got plenty of character references and so forth, so the probate judge should grant it right off. Then I'll tell you what to say in the letters, and I'll sign them. As the kids' legal guardian I'll have a lot more standing and we can maybe make these refusals final. How's that?"

"Oh, Geordie, we want to be *polite*——"

"What in time do you think I intend to do, threaten 'em with the police or something?" He sat back and glared at her, and then the tension of the long night and the bad dreams was broken, and they both laughed.

"It's a great idea," Lucy said. "I like it more and more."

Harold scratched at the door and Geordie got up and let him out. He stayed on the doorstep to be sure Harold didn't run off.

His brief triumph in the kitchen was gone as he remembered how Lucy looked when she said, "There's always something." It wasn't like her to be so cynical. When she wasn't worrying about Scott being sent away, she was probably wondering when they'd ever have a chance to get married. He ought to tell her to go ahead. But he didn't see how he could run the house when he was putting every spare minute into his work, trying desperately to get three steps ahead without sliding back three.

Harold came running back, as pleased to see Geordie as if he'd been gone a year. Geordie was reluctant to go back in and surprise that look in her face, and not be able to say anything. He smashed one fist into the other palm, ground it hard, then went inside again, saying briskly, "Looks like a day to haul tomorrow."

Lucy was more cheerful, to his relief. "And it's going to be a good day to take the twins to Limerock after school for shoes. They're practically curling their toes up now."

"You got enough money?"

"I've got a contribution from Penn. Imagine! Right out of his pocket when I just merely mentioned they'd need shoes soon. *And* the use of his car. He's leaving it home tomorrow for me."

"I wonder what he's up to now."

She smiled. "He may be growing up. . . . Look, it's almost two. I'm going back to bed."

11

Because Geordie didn't like surprises, Lucy told him that they were going to celebrate his twenty-first birthday and his guardianship in one party, and it would do him no good to object.

"Not a real party," she assured him. "But a special supper, with everything you like best. And there doesn't have to be anybody outside the family, if you don't want them. Not even Scott," she added.

"I can't let you make that sacrifice," said Geordie dryly. "Have Scott. But why all the fuss?"

"In books," said Lucy firmly, "reaching your twenty-first is known as attaining your majority. Doesn't that sound important enough for a celebration? And I think if we make a lot about your becoming the kids' guardian, it'll give them even more security. It sounds so protective."

"It's just a word," Geordie said. But he knew what it would do to his own doubts when he became legally the head of the family. From now on the family would be all that mattered. A man was lucky to have such a clear-cut purpose for his life, wasn't he? And to be undivided in it, to have no distractions?

He gave Lucy a cutting glance. "You got any more girls dredged up to spring on me at this celebration?"

"What do you mean 'any more'? I've never dredged up even one, which sounds as if I scooped them out of the clam flats with a steam shovel." She lifted her right hand solemnly. "On my honor as the Girl Scout I used to be I'm not springing anything on you."

"Not that one you tried to palm off on me at New Year's?"

"Never! She's back at college, anyway," Lucy added.

"*Good*. Let her be the sweetheart of Sigma Chi, or whatever it is."

On the day when Geordie was to be officially appointed guardian, he asked Lucy to go to court with him. Not that he needed her moral support, but he knew it would mean something to her. A few months ago, when he was merely the oldest boy of George Cameron and in love with Donna Blake, he wouldn't have been so sensitive as to what Lucy might feel and think.

After they left the probate judge's chambers, something seemed to be called for other than driving straight home. It was a fine soft day that felt like early spring, and here they were in Limerock in their best clothes.

"Let's get something to eat," Lucy suggested. "I was so nerved up I could hardly eat any dinner. Can we afford to eat out?"

"Sure! To heck with poverty! Throw the cat another herring!" His blue eyes were sparkling.

"It *does* make you feel different, doesn't it?"

"What gives you that idea?"   He took her elbow in a steely grip and pushed her toward the Crow's Nest.   She resisted for a moment, remembering that the last time she'd come in here she'd seen Penn and Shelley.   Then she gave in.   They ordered hot turkey sandwiches and ate with good appetite.   When they'd finished, and were waiting for apple pie for Geordie and chocolate pie for Lucy, she said, "How does it make you feel different?"

"As if something's ended, and I'm glad of it.   Something new's beginning.   It's a fresh start. . . .   What's ended is—listen, I don't mean life with Marm and Pa." He looked down at the table.   "But the time *since*.   I'm glad that's over with.   I was neither fish nor fowl nor good red herring.   Now I'm good for something."

Darn that Donna, she thought fiercely.   "You were always good for something.   A piece of paper doesn't make you *it*."

He smiled with one side of his mouth.   Whether he was pleased or being ironic she couldn't tell.

Lucy had planned the celebration dinner for the next night, so she could have all day to cook.   She spread the best tablecloth on the long kitchen table, and Genie set it with the flowered ironstone china that had miraculously been kept almost intact since their great-grandmother Sylvester received it as a wedding gift.   The twins were sent out for pussy willows and pine.   Scott provided the lobsters to be stuffed and baked.   There were baked potatoes, an immense green salad, hot rolls, and Boston cream pie, all Geordie's favorites.

Everyone dressed up, and behaved as if it were really an Occasion.   Afterwards they talked and sang until the younger ones were yawning, when they were sent to bed. Penn startled everyone by offering to help Genie with the dishes so that Lucy wouldn't have to do any more that night.

Geordie was pleased by the gesture. It showed that Penn still belonged to the family. "Scott, take Lucy out for a ride in the moonlight," he said. "She's been spinning like a top all day."

Lucy made a token objection, but she was as delighted as if he'd suggested a trip to Europe, and Scott stood there beaming on them all.

When they'd gone, Geordie went into the living room and turned the television on low. A movie about sheep farmers in Australia had just started, and Geordie lost himself at once in the story. Harold flopped at his feet with a long sigh.

Geordie was so absorbed in ranch life Down Under that it seemed no time at all before Genie put her head in and said, " 'Night, Geordie. Or are we supposed to call you *sir* now?"

He laughed. "Nope. *Your Excellency.* And get down and bump your forehead three times on the floor, and back out of my presence."

"Can I start tomorrow? I'm too sleepy tonight."

He waved a hand at her. "Dismissed. And thanks for all you did, Genie. It was a great party."

"Wasn't it?" She ran upstairs and he returned to the movie. When Penn came in he glanced up and said, "It's a good one. Filmed on location too. That's really Australia."

But after a moment he realized that Penn wasn't sitting down but was fiddling with things on the mantel. He remembered that once or twice during the evening he'd surprised an expression on Penn's face that had made him wonder if Penn were coming down with something. A commercial came on and he turned down the sound.

"You all right? You've been looking kind of uneasy all evening, when you thought nobody was noticing you."

"But you noticed, right?" Penn's laugh was forced. It died in the effort. He ran his tongue over his lips and the words burst out. "You got to be twenty-one just in time. I want to get married, and you'll have to sign for me."

Geordie's first reaction was an astonishment so great it almost amounted to admiration for Penn's nerve. "Married!" he said at last. "I'm surprised you didn't find a way to manage that on your own, the way you run the rest of your business."

"Don't think I haven't tried to manage it," said Penn bitterly. "But I couldn't figure out how to fake a birth certificate." Then he tried to grin. "How about it, Geordie?"

"For Pete's sake! You think you can walk in and say I want to get married, like the twins saying, Can we have a quarter? and I'll say, Yes, like handing over the quarter?" Geordie got up so violently that Harold arose too, gazed reproachfully at Geordie's feet, and moved to a different spot. "I couldn't make you apply for college. I couldn't keep you from getting that car, I can't keep you in nights short of knocking you out and tying you to the bed. But I can keep you from getting married before you're out of high school, and brother, I will!"

Penn was standing too. He was pale, and his eyes were oddly shiny. "I have to get married," he said. "She's going to have a b-b——" He stammered uncontrollably on the last word and finally gave up. The two brothers stood staring at each other. Geordie felt as if the boom of his jigger sail had caught him on the side of his head and knocked him out, but somehow he was still standing up with his eyes open. Now it was Penn's turn to say "You all right?"

"Why shouldn't I be?" he said harshly. "I'm not the one to disgrace the family. Maybe it's a good thing Marm and Pa are both dead, so they don't have to know about this."

"You can say what you want, call me everything you can put tongue to, but it doesn't change anything. I've got to get married, and you have to give your consent."

"I don't *have* to do anything," said Geordie. "And I won't. You're too young to get married, and that's that." He leaned over and turned up the television and gazed at the action on the screen without seeing it.

"Listen, Geordie," said Penn at his elbow. "I want to be with her when she tells them, so I can tell them it's all right, we can get married right away."

"Oh, is *that* supposed to make it all right?" asked Geordie. "Never mind what you two have been up to, you can get married and that makes you just the same as the ones who wait. And what gives you the idea the Searses will be crazy about having you marry their daughter?"

101

"It's what she wants," said Penn, "and that'll be okay with them. Sure, they won't be happy about her getting in trouble, but it'd be worse if she tried to do something about stopping it."

Geordie turned off the television. *"No,"* he said quietly, though he felt anything but quiet. He had to put his hands in his pockets to keep from grabbing Penn and shaking him till his eyes crossed. "I know how you figgered this, just how you worked it. You must have had your eye on Sears' girl for a long time and now you think you've got her, and everything else along with her. Is that it? You'll be a partner in the business before you can spit, and you'll get it all without any work, unless it was work to make her fall for you."

Penn had gone very red. As the color ebbed away he seemed white in contrast. He was holding his lower lip down with his teeth and his eyes were almost shut.

"That's how it is, isn't it?" Geordie goaded him. "College is a lot of hard work. But get a nice girl into trouble, and you'd be all set. You're using her and your own kid to get ahead! Well, they don't need *you*, Penn. Her folks can look after them, and you can make it on your own, the hard way, like the rest of us."

Penn turned and walked out of the room. Geordie heard him leave the house and in a few minutes the car engine was racing, and then it went out of the yard. He went outside and listened as the car went up the lane entirely too fast. Silence meant it had reached the main road and gone around the first bend.

Geordie felt uneasy in his stomach. He assured himself that the roads were dry and there'd be very little traffic on them at this hour. He tried not to think of all the empty stretches where a car could go off the road and no one would know until someone drove that way in the morning.

His head felt icy-cold, his forehead was wet with sweat. If the boy killed himself tonight, would it be *his* fault for saying no? He shook his head savagely. Blasted kid anyway, tearing off in a tantrum the minute he couldn't get his own way.

He went back into the house. All the assurance he had felt earlier, the vigor of a fresh start, had gone. Standing in the silent kitchen he felt the cry rising inside him, never to be uttered but a cry nonetheless. *Pa! Marm! Come back!*

12

I T HAD BEEN a lovely ride. They'd met practically no other cars; they had been alone in a silver world of common houses made uncommon by moonlight, familiar woods turned into enchanted forests, well-known fields become the mysterious slopes of an unknown planet. They parked for a while at a deserted beach and watched the moonlight on the sea, and the surf sparkling around the rocks.

It was the perfect close to a perfect day. "Geordie's right," Lucy said. "It's a new start. We can't keep looking back and wishing things were different. We have to go ahead."

"You said anything to him yet about our plans?" Scott asked.

"No, he's had so many other things on his mind. . . . Oh, *you* know," she said apologetically. "I want him to get over Donna some more, maybe meet somebody else. And anyway, I want to wait till Genie's had her fifteenth birthday. That'll be in April. Maybe then we can see an actual date in sight." She sighed, and snuggled deeper into Scott's arm. "Just thinking of spring makes everything seem more hopeful. They keep passing you over for the draft, so maybe you won't be called. . . . I keep thinking."

"I wouldn't mind going if it wasn't for you," he said seriously. "I'd enlist and get it over with."

"Well, if I'm an *inconvenience*, Mr. Barstow——"

He laughed and kissed her. "I should've enlisted before I fell in love."

"Well, I just have a feeling you won't be called. Our love is casting strange influences on the draft board."

When they drove into the yard at Cameron Point, Penn's car was gone, and just one small light showed in the house, in the kitchen. They kissed good night, Scott left, and Lucy went happily and drowsily to bed.

Geordie had already left the house when she came down in the morning. Going to the front door for her daily view of the cove and the weather, she saw *Mary C.* heading out, and waved though she knew Geordie wasn't looking. It was more of a salutation to the day and their future. When he'd urged her and Scott out last night he'd looked better than he had for months, and his new confidence showed in the note he'd left at her place on the table, scribbled in a hurry.

"Write and tell them the kids can visit next week. Call up if you feel like it, we can afford it this time. Get it over with."

She smiled to herself. Apparently he no longer felt the visit would be a threat. Well, she didn't either, for some reason.

On school mornings Penn was usually up ahead of the younger ones so as to have the bathroom to himself, but today they were all up ahead of him. Finally Lucy went up to see what was wrong.

He was awake, staring glassily at the ceiling. "Are you sick?" she asked him.

"Yeah," he muttered. "I can't make it to school today." He groaned and rolled over to face the wall. "You call Shelley, huh? Tell her I'm sick, and I'll see her tonight if I can."

"I hope it isn't the flu," Lucy said. "We've all been lucky so far this year." She leaned anxiously over the footboard. "Do you feel hot? Do your bones ache?"

"I just feel lousy." He kept his eyes closed. "All over. No particular place." He pulled the covers over his head. "Just call Shelley. 0548."

"Maybe it's because you stayed out so late last night," she said hopefully, and left him. Who was it said the other day that this was pneumonia weather?

In the kitchen she hushed the others and dialed the Sears' number. She felt very uncomfortable. What if she got Mrs. Sears? Lucy concentrated on Great-grand-father Cameron and those university degrees, and when someone answered she said with dignity, "May I speak to Shelley?"

"This is Shelley." The voice was soft and rather breathless.

"Oh, hi, Shelley," said Lucy more naturally. "This is Lucy Cameron. I'm calling for Penn. He doesn't feel well this morning, so he's still in bed. But he'll see you tonight if he feels better."

"Oh . . ." The word trailed off. Then even more softly Shelley said, "Well, thank you very much." There was another silence, then Shelley said faintly, "Good-bye."

"Good-bye," Lucy hung up. Goodness! Shelley was so much in love with Penn, poor kid, that not to ride to school with him this morning was a disaster. "Who hasn't brushed their teeth yet?" she called. "Who's got a library book to take? Who hasn't got a handkerchief?"

When they had gone at last, sunny tranquillity settled over Cameron Point. Harold came back down the lane and lay on the front doorstep in the sun. The birds chattered, crows called. Lucy, feeling very sophisticated, made a long-distance call to Aunt Nora Sylvester in Massachusetts and said the twins could come.

"You don't know what this will mean to us, Lucy," Aunt Nora said.

"I know how you and Uncle Bill feel about the boys," Lucy said. "But we can't possibly give them up. We all belong together. I wouldn't want you to think we might change our minds. . . . I mean, it wouldn't be fair to you. So if that's understood——"

"If you're willing to share them with us we're grateful, dear. . . . Bill and I will drive down for the children on Saturday. Pray for fine weather. Oh, and would Genie like to come? Because we'd love to have her. Will you ask her?"

"I will," Lucy promised. As she turned away from the telephone, relieved and thinking about a second breakfast before she tackled the work, she came face to face with Penn. He was dressed, but looked ghastly.

"Want something to eat?" she asked.

He grimaced. "No. I've got a propeller going in my stomach."

She brought a bowl of cereal to the table for herself. "I ate once, but I never know what I'm eating with those twins going strong after a night's rest. This is my real breakfast."

Suddenly Penn said in a choked voice, "You've got to talk to him, Luce. He won't let me marry Shelley, and I have to."

Her head rang as if she'd been violently slapped. She could feel her face going cold as the blood left it. Penn's face was white too. "You mean a *baby?*" she whispered, and he nodded. He began talking through the ringing in her ears.

"She hasn't told them yet. I'm supposed to be with her when she does. I never thought Geordie'd hold out. I thought he'd cuss me, call me everything, but still sign." His mouth twisted up on one side. "He cussed me all right and he called me everything, and he won't sign. What do I *do,* Luce? For Pete's sake, isn't there anybody else who'll let me do it?" He went quickly to a window and stood looking out.

No wonder Shelley had sounded so faint and breathless on the telephone. Lucy said, breathless herself, "Penn, all I can do is try to find out why Geordie says no."

"Oh, he'll tell you all right," he said bitterly without looking around. "He told me. In detail."

"It must have been a terrible shock to him. It is to me. Oh, Penn!" she exclaimed in anger and grief. "How could you do it? It's bad enough for us older ones, but Genie will be so ashamed, and if any of the younger ones get hold of it——"

He swung around. "Oh, knock it off! I know all about the shame and the disgrace and all the rest of the guff. But there wouldn't be any if that stiff-necked, moralizing Puritan would say the word. We'd be married in a week and nobody could prove anything, no matter how much they talked!"

"I'll do the best I can," she promised him, or was it herself? She hugged herself against a sudden chill.

"Thanks," he muttered, and grabbed up his jacket from the back of a chair. Then she saw his books piled on one end of the counter. "I might as well go to school. I'll go crazy around here today." On the way out he stopped. "Uh—what did Shelley say?"

A fine time to think of Shelley. She said coldly, "She said 'Oh,' and then 'Thank you very much' and then 'Good-bye.' She'll probably be glad to see you today."

"Yeah," he muttered. "But I'd rather be shot." He shut the door on the last word. She watched him hurry across the yard to his car, shoulders hunched and dark head bent, and she was both sorry for him and furious with him. When he'd driven away, she gave Harold her oatmeal and fixed herself a cup of tea which did little for her. Still, as the shock waves died away, she was able to think more clearly, and she tried to imagine the scene that had taken place here while she'd been out in the moonlight with Scott. She felt like weeping with dismay, both for herself and for Geordie. Penn's confession must have hit him right between the eyes.

That must be why he'd refused his consent, in the first

reaction against Penn's behavior. When he came in from hauling today he'd have changed his mind. But now she knew why the children could go away for a week, so they'd be out of the way and not overhear anything they shouldn't. Probably when they got back Penn would be married and out of the house. . . .

Penn married. Penn out of the house for good, at seventeen!

She was halfway to the telephone to call Scott before she stopped herself. She couldn't tell him over the wire, and she couldn't ask him to leave off packing lobsters and come to her. But she had to do something to fill up the hours until Geordie came home and they could get at it.

The twins' clothes for their trip. That was it. She ran up the stairs and Harold loped after her, choosing to think it was a magnificent game of tag.

~~~~~~

13

S OMETIMES it breezed up by noon and forced Geordie in early, but this was one of the calm, gemlike days of which there were far too few in winter, and Lucy knew she wouldn't see Geordie home until dark.

It was one of the worst days she had spent since her mother died. But of course this time the twins weren't upset too, and they came home from school bursting with noise and energy. Ralph came home with Genie, and instead of going prowling they decided to study at the kitchen table.

"Ralph, does your mother know you're here?" Lucy asked sharply.

"Why, yes," he said, looking hurt and innocent.

Saying she had a headache, which was the truth, Lucy went up to her room and tried to read. The house re-sounded with yelps of youthful vigor, mysterious crashes, running feet, Harold's barking, Genie's threats, and Ralph's whoops of laughter. At least they were all happy, Lucy thought drearily, and at this point she couldn't care less what happened to the house as long as they didn't set it on fire.

She actually fell asleep for a time, and when she woke up the twilight was blue against the windows and the house was silent. Hastily she put on her shoes and brushed her hair and went downstairs. The twins were watching a television western, turned low, and in the kitchen Genie was finishing up her homework. *Music to Dream By* was playing on her Christmas record player.

"Where is everybody?" Lucy asked.

"Ralph's gone home and Geordie's been in, and gone back to the fishhouse." Genie looked up from her notebook, scowling. "And is *he* cranky! He wouldn't let the twins go down with him. I don't think he likes being twenty-one and the official head of the family!"

"Oh, he probably didn't get very many lobsters, that's all." Lucy pulled on her boots and the wool shirt, and went out. Harold ran ahead of her down the path. When she went into the lighted fishhouse, Geordie was sitting on a nail keg by the woodstove, his elbows on his knees, his head in his hands.

She said right away, "Penn told me this morning. Geordie, *why?*"

"Ask him." He got up and went to the workbench.

"No, I meant why won't you sign?"

He turned on her, his eyes blazing. "Listen, you know as well as I do what the score is. He thought he was doing pretty well for himself. He's a conniving little chiseler, that's what our brother is."

"You think he planned this?" she asked faintly.

"I *do*." He brought the hammer down hard.

"If I believed that, I'd never want to speak to Penn again." Her eyes filled with tears. "He was sick this

112

morning. He looked awful. I think he's scared stiff that Mr. Sears will have him arrested or something. And what about Shelley? She's worse off. **. . .** I know how *I'd* feel." She sat down dejectedly.

"I'm sorry for her," Geordie said curtly, "but she's not our affair. And look, we aren't talking about this at all while the kids are in the house. That's why I said they could go. If old man Sears shows up here with the sheriff, I don't want them around."

"You think he will?" She jumped up again in panic, as if the sheriff were already there, with a posse.

"How the heck do I know what they can do? It's going to be a rotten mess, and Penn'll still say everybody else is to blame."

"I've got to go start supper," said Lucy wildly, and left him. Her throat aching as she fought back tears, she made up her mind to call Scott and ask him to come that evening. Only the sight of him could restore her.

He couldn't offer any concrete help. "No, I won't talk to Geordie," he said. "Might be he's right. And it's not my business. He's running this family, and he wouldn't appreciate me butting in."

"But what are we going to *do*? It used to be every time the telephone rang I thought you'd got your draft notice. Now I think it's the Searses. Or their lawyer," she added shakily. They were sitting on the stairs in the front hall, trying for privacy, and Scott pulled her snugly into his arm.

"Look, Penn's a minor, and he's no more to blame than she is. So I don't know what the law can do. But I promise you one thing. You're going to live through it."

"But I'd like to live a little easier," she said. "Everything is such a hard grind. It's like one bad dream after another, without waking up in between. And if I do feel happy for a day, I know Geordie's *un*happy."

He kissed her. "Geordie'll survive too. You'll see. He's still growing up, you know, even if he is twenty-one. He'll learn how to handle things. And Penn will land on his feet."

"While I'm listening to you, I believe you," she said. And it was the truth. The doubts always came in the door when Scott left.

When she told the twins that they were going to Boston on a visit, their whoops seemed to bounce off the rafters.

"How come Geordie changed his mind?" Genie asked.

Lucy said carelessly, "I guess he thought it would be a nice thing for them, after all."

"Geordie's some glum these days," Genie muttered. "It's that darn' Donna." Penn was away from home so much that Genie hadn't yet sensed the tension between him and Geordie.

Friday after school Geordie trimmed the twins' hair. "I wish you were going too, Genie," he told her with a sincerity that Lucy understood; she too wished Genie could be out of earshot for a while.

"Well, it would be kind of nice to see Boston," Genie said, "but Marcie's lending me her bike while she's visiting her cousin in Portland, and Ralph and I have plans. If only it doesn't snow." She crossed her fingers.

Saturday was cold but fair. Geordie went out to haul. When the Sylvesters arrived their smiles were visible from the instant the car turned out of the lane. Lucy had lunch ready, and everything went well until they were about to leave, when Philip disappeared. Everyone thought he was in the bathroom, but after a while it became clear that he wasn't.

Lucy ran upstairs and found him sitting on his bed, looking out at the sparkling blue cove. His small shoulders were slumped. She thought in panic, What if he says he won't go? I can't make him, and then what about Peter? Shall I let him go alone? . . . What would Marm do?

She sat down beside Philip, who stared harder out the window. "Homesick already, Pip?" she asked.

"Why'd Geordie go out today?"

"Because it's not very windy, and he has to catch any good weather that comes along."

"I sh'd think," Philip began. He gulped, and blinked very rapidly. "I sh'd think it'd be important to say good-bye to *us!* We never went away before and it's not like just going to Limerock."

The twins had transferred to Geordie the adoration they'd felt for their father, and now the strength of that worship struck her hard. It had begun on the night he'd roared in this room, "Come aboard and bring your dory!"

She put her arm around Philip. "Know what? I wasn't supposed to tell you this because he wanted to surprise you. But he's going to call you and Peter up tonight. Your own long-distance telephone call!"

His eyes were luminous and not just from tears. *"Honest!* Hey, when? We want to be sure to be there!"

"Seven o'clock," she said firmly. "You tell Uncle Bill that you're expecting a call at seven o'clock." And Geordie'd darn well better call up too, she thought grimly. She got up. "Come on, blow your nose, give me a hug, and let's go." He gave her a half-strangling hug and ran out of the room ahead of her.

They were gone, and the silence seemed to throb. Harold came and laid his head in Lucy's lap, looking worried. She said, "They'll be back, if you can just survive a week with no hugs and kisses."

"I'd just as soon hug him, but no kisses," said Genie. "Gosh, this place is empty! Look, as soon as we do the dishes will you drive me over to Marcie's to get her bike? Ralph and I are going out on Burying Point and look for arrowheads."

They took Harold with them in the pickup, because he looked so sad. After Lucy let Genie off, she considered not going back home. There was nothing to go home for. Oh, she could always find some chore that needed doing, but the thought of the empty house sitting above an empty cove in the winter sunshine oppressed her. But where would she go? The friends with whom she'd gone to school would all have plans for such a fine Saturday afternoon. Scott was busy getting a big shipment of lobsters ready to go out.

Reluctantly she headed the truck toward home.

The old house and big barn had an abandoned look, as if some mysterious disaster had taken the people away all at once. Lucy slammed the pickup door hard when she and Harold got out, and began talking to him in a loud cheerful voice. "We've got to think about the garden, Harold, and order the seeds this week. And I was wondering about chickens. Wouldn't they make a nice sound around the place? We always used to have hens. I loved to go out and gather the eggs. Would you be good to our hens, Harold?"

Harold looked benign, and she laughed. "I know, you only chase seagulls. . . . Now another thing I've thought about, Harold, is goats. Goat's milk is very nutritious, and if anybody could hear me now they'd say I'd flipped. Think of all the times I've wanted to just *yell,* and couldn't. Well, now I can yell without scaring the hide off anybody."

She began to sing *The Battle Hymn of the Republic* and marched into the house leading an imaginary band. Harold pranced and applauded. "Glory, glory, hallelujah!" she sang, and finished with a drawn-out, impressive, "His soul goes—marching—*on.*"

Harold sang the last note with her in a long quavering soprano, and then went into transports of delight and nearly knocked her down. Laughing, she hugged him, dodging his tongue. Then suddenly he sprang toward the back door, barking.

It was Penn and Shelley. Penn grinned at her. "Sounds like a concert in here."

"It was," she said. "Harold and me in a duet. We're going on the stage as soon as I teach him to play the guitar. Hi, Shelley. Come on in." She was shaky, and it occurred to her that they were all shaky, for one reason

117

or another. Shelley leaned down to pat Harold as if to hide self-consciousness, and Penn's grin wasn't a happy one.

"I thought Geordie'd be in by now."

"You know Geordie. He stays out till the sunset gun." She put the tea kettle forward on the stove. "Take Shelley's things, Penn. Gosh, am I glad to see company. This house is some empty with the kids gone."

Shelley didn't want to give up her coat. She perched on a chair like a cold and frightened bird, ready to fly at the first quick movement. Her long fair hair fell down over her collar, pale as cornsilk, and under her bangs her eyes were unexpectedly a light golden-brown instead of blue. Frightened eyes; in spite of the makeup, they reminded Lucy of Harold's eyes when he was worried or in pain. Shelley seemed just that helpless.

Penn fidgeted around the kitchen, picking things up and putting them down. Lucy felt worse and worse. At first she'd been glad her parents had been spared Penn's trouble. Now she knew they'd have managed it, as parents almost always manage. But she wasn't even two years older than Penn!

She said desperately, "Look, you two——" Shelley's head came up, and Lucy shook hers. "The kids have just gone, and now we'll have a chance to thrash things out. . . . If you can just be patient."

"We can't wait much longer," Shelley said in her soft voice. "We've got to tell them, or else I——" The words died away. The hand caressing Harold's ear shook visibly.

Penn said hoarsely, "It'll be Geordie's fault if anything goes wrong. You just tell him that."

A cold little breeze of anger stirred in Lucy. "Is it his fault, Penn? You sure of that? Wasn't it somebody else's fault, a while back? I'm sorry, Shelley, but it's pretty unrealistic to blame everything on Geordie."

"I know that," said Shelley, quite strongly. She lifted her chin out of her collar. "I'm not blaming anybody for the fix I'm in, and I'd get out of it myself if I could. Maybe I will yet. But the more I think about the baby, the more I want it." She gave Penn a quick glance and then looked down again, and her hair half-veiled her face.

Penn, Lucy wanted to shout at him, why don't you go stand beside her, even if you don't touch her? Can't you see how alone she is, or are you only interested in saving your own skin? But Penn looked frozen in his tracks.

"Shelley, I know you hate to tell your parents, but you should, right away. Don't do anything foolish on your own, *please*. Never mind about Penn or Geordie, but tell your mother and get it over with. And I promise you I'll keep at Geordie, I won't give him a minute's peace."

"Well . . ." Shelley got up as if she already felt heavy.

"Let's have a good hot cup of something," Lucy urged.

"Thank you, but I couldn't eat anything," Shelley said. "I'm so nervous I——" Her voice trembled. Her hair hiding her face, she turned hurriedly toward the door. With a glance at Lucy that cut like knives Penn went after her. Lucy knew the wound was not meant for her but for the cruel surprise of his own behavior kicking him brutally in the face. Suddenly she felt years older and thought, Ah, we're hard on him and he's only a child after all.

14

GEORDIE was bone-tired when he came in, and she couldn't start in on him at once. When she told him the children were expecting him to call, he gave her a weary grin.

"You're kind of reckless, aren't you?" he asked. "Acting like we're millionaires with these long-distance calls."

"It'll be worth a million to them and to you too," she retorted. "If you could have seen poor Pip!"

Then Genie came home, excited by her afternoon. She had a pocket full of felsite pieces: broken knives and points and scrapers, and one prize carried cautiously in a pocket by itself. An unbroken, still sharp, dark red spear point. Even Geordie was impressed, and got out the old magnifying glass to examine the fine workmanship along the edges.

"Ralph says it's probably been right there ever since some Indian threw a spear to kill a moose or something hundreds of years ago!" Genie said. "And it just got washed out of the bank when the frost started to go and it rained so hard last week."

"Sounds likely," Geordie agreed. Proudly Genie put

the spear point up in front of the mantel clock, and then sat down to study the other pieces.

After supper there was no chance to bring up Penn and Shelley, with Genie right there. While they were doing the dishes Genie said, "Ralph says Donna's going around with a boy whose father's president of the bank. Ralph's father knows him. Ralph says this boy's lost his license for drunken driving, and Donna has to drive him everywhere. Boy! And I bet she thinks she's doing pretty good for herself because his father's a banker. *Yuck!*"

"What's that for?" said Geordie, coming into the kitchen.

"Oh, I was just telling Lucy about some boy," said Genie glibly.

"Well, it's time to call the kids," said Geordie. "So stop yakking for five minutes."

The twins were full of things to tell him, and he was very patient, letting them get out the most unbearably exciting news before he told them to save the rest till they got home. Lucy and Genie had to speak to them too. Then Geordie told them they were to mind their manners and brush their teeth and be a credit to the family.

When the calls were over he said he was going to bed and read. Lucy supposed she could go up in a little while and talk to him in his room. But she was a coward, she admitted it freely; and if they got all worked up tonight neither of them would sleep much.

Tomorrow morning, she promised herself. First thing. No, as soon as Genie goes to Sunday school. Penn called later in the evening and said he was spending the night with a school friend in Limerock. So he'd be out of the way too.

Sunday was another fine morning of false spring. Genie was off early on the borrowed bicycle, her good clothes in the carrier. She'd change at a friend's house for Sunday school.

Geordie was working on gear, so Lucy put doughnuts in the oven to heat, then wrapped them up and took them and a pitcher of milk down to the fishhouse. Instead of mending traps, Geordie had hauled a skiff into the middle of the floor and was scraping the blistered paint off it.

As usual she surprised a somber expression on his face before he had time to change it for her. "What's all this?"

"Time for a mug-up. *And* a talk." She sounded more confident than she really was. "Maybe a fight. But I'm ready for it."

He opened his mouth and she shook her head. "Have a hot doughnut first." She poured out milk for him. "No matter what, you've got to eat and keep your strength up."

"That your sermon for today?"

"Nope, it's advice for both of us. We're going to live through this the way we've lived through some pretty awful things that were a lot worse." She just hoped Scott was right.

They ate the warm doughnuts and drank the cold milk, watching the flashing, choppy cove and *Mary C.* dancing on her mooring. "What are you going to do with the skiff?" Lucy asked him. "Sell her?"

"No. It's for the twins to use this summer. What's the sense of being a kid on the coast if you don't have a boat? They're old enough to learn how to handle one."

"Make them wear life preservers, though."

"Oh, sure, but they'll be insulted." They swapped understanding smiles, then Geordie said suddenly, "You want to talk about Penn, right?"

"Yes, and please hear me out, Geordie." She looked pleadingly into his eyes, and finally he nodded. "He brought Shelley here yesterday. I know how you feel about Penn, I feel the same way. But she's something different, Geordie. She's the one who'll really have to pay, and she's so frightened she's pathetic."

"Poor little rich girl," said Geordie.

"You said you'd hear me out."

He shrugged and went back to scraping paint. There was something about the back of his head and the set of his shoulders that drained off her confidence, but she struggled on.

"Geordie, if you say okay now it'll all be off your hands. We don't *have* Penn, so we're not losing him. We ought to get on with our own lives and let him sink or swim in his."

He sat back on his heels and looked up at her. "Can't you get this through your skull, or are you stupid? I can't write him off! He's one of us. Marm and Pa expected us older ones to bring up the younger ones, and I can't let Penn get away with this. If he doesn't learn now he'll never learn, and what'll he amount to?" His cheekbones flushed and his voice grew hoarse as if his throat had tightened up. "They expected him to amount to something, Luce. They were sure of it. And by god-frey, he's *going* to, or else!"

She was shaken by his outburst. But she could still say bitterly, "Or else what?"

Outside, Harold burst into a wild fanfare. She looked through the window that faced the house and saw a car cautiously navigating the soft ruts. "Who's that?"

Geordie stood up and looked. "That's Martin Sears out slumming in his Cadillac. Too bad he didn't get mired in the lane." He dropped the paint scraper on the bench and strode out.

Harold was still cheering the car on. It came to a stop in the drive before the front door but Mr. Sears, intimi-dated by Harold, didn't get out. Geordie was already halfway up the slope, and Lucy ran out and caught up with him. She'd be beside him to meet the attack. Ei-ther they'd be told that Penn was a vicious delinquent who should be in jail, or that Geordie was something worse for withholding consent.

"Come here, Harold!" Geordie called and the dog came bounding to him, telling him about the stranger. "Ayuh, that's all right now," Geordie said. "You stay with me." They walked up to the car.

The first astonishing thing was Mr. Sears' smile. He was a thickset, ruddy man with fair hair and blue eyes, and his smile was broad. "Is it safe to get out?" he called.

"Yes," Geordie answered, unsmiling. Mr. Sears got out and Harold went to him, wagging, ears laid back, and was patted.

"Well, Geordie and Lucy," Mr. Sears put his hand

125

out, and when Geordie didn't move Lucy walked forward and shook hands with him. "I miss that smile of yours when I walk through the plant, Lucy," he said. "I'm sorry about your folks. I didn't know your mother, but George Cameron was a fine man."

"Thank you," Lucy said, wishing that Geordie would at least remember his manners even if he didn't want to talk. "Won't you come in?" she asked, and led the way to the front door. She was relieved when Geordie followed.

As she stopped at the sitting-room door, Mr. Sears said, "Couldn't we go into the kitchen? Somehow I always feel better in a kitchen."

They went into the kitchen and she pushed forward the captain's chair for Mr. Sears. She sat down, and Geordie leaned against the counter.

"Well," said Mr. Sears, turning less cheerful. "We know about Shelley. She was crying in the night and my wife just happened to wake up and hear her, so she went in to her, and——" He lifted his hands in a helpless gesture. "Naturally this is a shock, but I'm not going into details as to how her mother and I felt last night, and how we feel now. Shelley's alive, she hasn't tried anything foolish, and we've got to make the best of it."

Lucy, feeling very hot, wished she could look away, but she had to keep her eyes on his face and show her courage. Geordie might be in the room, but he was no help.

"I didn't come to make trouble this morning," Mr. Sears went on. "I was out driving around, trying to settle down, and it came to me that you two youngsters must be feeling pretty upset too. Is Penn here?"

Lucy shook her head and tried to moisten her lips.

"Well, I'll see him later. Now I know how you two are trying to keep the family together and raise the younger ones, and I admire you for it. So I just wanted to tell you not to worry. Shelley's been drifting through life, never acting particularly happy till this last year when she stayed home and went to school here. She really loves it around here and that pleases me, you can bet. Her mother——" He cleared his throat and looked down at his feet. "Well, you have to have roots in a place like this to love it. I can't blame *her*. But Shelley, she's a Sears of Port George, no doubt about it. And it might be that she's cut out to be a good wife and mother, and we've had to find out the hard way."

He stopped and cleared his throat again. "Would you have some coffee?" Lucy said instantly. He smiled at her and shook his head. "I've been drinking coffee since two this morning."

"Milk then?"

"Well——"

She sprang up to get it. Anything to put off the moment when he demanded Geordie's consent, and Geordie refused.

"Penn's a bright boy, and an ambitious one. But Shelley says he doesn't want to go to college, he thinks it's time wasted. Well, I didn't go to college either, in fact I didn't finish high school, but I went into the fish-packing business at fifteen when old Pomeroy owned it.

Now I own it, and it's a lot bigger now than old Pomeroy ever dreamed it could be. And I did it all."

He sat back in the captain's chair and said expansively, "I plan to put Penn right into the factory as soon as he graduates and have him learn the business from the ground up, or should I say from the ocean up?" He sipped the cold milk. "You won't have to worry about that boy. He'll go far."

"He already has," said Geordie. "Too far. We're not proud of him."

"Now, son, it takes two, and I'm not holding him a bit more responsible than Shelley. So don't you be too hard on him. You'll be proud of him sometime." He finished the milk and stood up. "That was good, Lucy. I feel better, both from that and from talking to you two."

"I feel better too," said Lucy quite honestly, until it dawned on her that Shelley had simply let her parents think the marriage was unopposed.

"Shelley and her mother'll get together on the wedding as soon as they feel better," he said. "They're both pretty worn out this morning and sleeping it off. They'll get in touch with you, Lucy." He went over to Geordie and put out his hand. "Come on, son, relax. Remember that useful motto, 'It could be worse.' "

"It's Lucy's motto too," said Geordie dryly, and relented enough to shake hands.

When Mr. Sears had gone Lucy said, "Well, I didn't hear you telling him what you'd just been telling me."

"I kept trying to think of a way to start off," said Geordie, "but I was scared either my voice wouldn't

128

come out or it would squeak. Steam roller, that's what he is."

"He was nice. Oh, Geordie, give in!"

"No!" he roared. He strode up and down the kitchen, waving his arms. "You hear him? They're going to be rewarded! That's all right, bless your little hearts, you just had to do it because Shelley, she wants to be a mama and play house, and Penn doesn't want to waste time in college, he wants to be a big man like Martin Sears, so give 'em everything!"

"I don't see it that way," Lucy protested. "Just because Shelley's father happens to be who he is——"

"Happens to be! That's why he picked Shelley! And he thinks he can get away with it!" He stalked out of the house. Lucy went up to her room and gave in wholeheartedly to her tears, while Harold sat on the rug beside her bed and worried.

15

DINNER WAS a silent meal. Lucy announced brightly that she was going for a long walk around the shore, and Genie seized eagerly on that. They both looked at Geordie, who said without premeditation, "I planned on looking for some stuff in the attic while the coast was clear. When the kids get up there with me, I can't put my mind on anything."

When the girls and Harold had gone, he went up the back stairs to the attic. It was warm and dry up there under the roof, with the sun coming in at the windows, and the only sounds the small mysterious ones of an old house. In a bad storm you could come up here and hear the house creaking like a ship at sea, and if you put your hands up on the hand-hewn beams they seemed to be as alive as they'd once been in the forest.

At one end of the long attic the boys' trains were set up. There was a sagging couch pulled up to a window and some old magazines dropped down beside it. That meant Genie. Geordie lay down on the couch, punched the cushions into shape under his head, and stared out at the sunlit green spruce tops moving lightly against the sky. A crow sat on one jeering down at something. Chickadees flashed back and forth. Spring looked very close today.

He didn't think very much. He was tired of thinking. He felt detached up here and there was something restful about the silence. It was as if everything had stopped for a little while, even time.

When he heard something different he thought the wind was rising. It always made queer noises up around the eaves and the chimneys. When it turned into footsteps on the back stairs, he thought it was one of the girls come back to tell him about something they'd found on the shore. Maybe a skiff drifting in.

With a sigh he sat up. . . . Still, Genie'd be running up the stairs, and these feet came slow. Curious in spite of himself, he waited for them to reach the top and for the door to be opened.

Penn stood there. "Hi," he said wanly.

"I didn't hear the car."

"She's in the Bay Garage uptown. She got water in her gas, somehow. Buzz brought me down, as far as the mailbox." He shut the door behind him, walked halfway toward Geordie, and stopped where the train tracks began. "Hey, what would we have thought, getting electric trains for Christmas?"

"I don't recollect ever wanting them."

"Nope, it was always boats for you. But I can remember wanting trains so bad I could taste it. I drooled, thinking about a locomotive. I used to put myself to sleep building whole villages, farms and all, for the tracks to run by. I was going to be the only boy in

Maine with one whole mile of track." He laughed. *"One—whole—mile,* all turns and twists. People would come from everywhere to see my setup. The Camerons would be famous."

He stepped across the loops of track and sat down in an old armchair.

"How'd you know I was here?" Geordie asked.

"The door was open at the foot of the stairs when I came into the back entry. So I came up to look. I wasn't sure you were here," he admitted.

"Well, I am." Geordie's restful detachment was gone, and he might as well go find something to do in the fish-house, before they got fighting again. Because Penn hadn't come up here just to reminisce about wanting electric trains. He started to get up and Penn said, "Can I talk to you?"

"I don't know as we've got much to say," said Geordie.

"Maybe you haven't, but I have." He sounded tightened up, almost too much to breathe. "I should've said it before, but I was so shook up I couldn't get started."

"Well?" Geordie watched him.

"You think I planned this. That I'm just using Shelley to get myself a good berth with Sears, so I'll be fixed for life with no sweat." He sat forward, staring into Geordie's face. "It's not true. Sure, I felt pretty good about dating Shelley Sears. She's been a lot of places and met a lot of people. When she started going to Limerock High nobody could get near her, and first they figured she was stuck-up. Then the girls said she wasn't, she was shy, she had a real inferiority complex because

132

she thought nobody would like her on account of her money."

He laughed nervously. "It was a challenge, I guess. It took me a while, but finally she went out with me. I thought I could let it go after a few dates. I know girls that are a lot more fun from the start. Only thing was——" His voice was unsteady. "I couldn't drop her. I was hooked, and she never even tried. She just *is*, like a flower with brains." He tried to laugh again.

Visions of Donna tormented Geordie. He cleared his throat. "What do you mean, hooked?"

"I love her," Penn said huskily, and went dark red. "I mean it, Geordie. It's just about turned me inside out. I never had any idea it would be like this. And she loves me. Do you think we'd have gone that far if it *wasn't* love? Not her! And not me either! I never planned to get into this kind of mess." Wiping his forehead he said intensely, "Only it's not a mess when you're in love. The other people make the mess."

"Other people meaning me," said Geordie dryly. "Strikes me you're kind of young to know about love. Isn't that just an excuse for your actions? Calling it love?"

"It's love," said Penn doggedly, "when I can't stand to see her cry. Not that she cries much around me, but when she's trying not to that's worse. I want to take on the whole world for her, Geordie, and what I feel is a man's feelings, but you treat me like a little kid." His voice dropped almost to a whisper. "I could kill you for it."

"Listen," Geordie said, "you've got your feelings to

133

wrassle with and I've got mine. You're my younger brother, and I'm responsible for you. I have to decide what's best for you. And I don't think marriage at seventeen is *it*. First, you don't know how deep your feelings and hers really go. Six months from now maybe you can't stand the sight of each other. And second, how fit are you to start being a husband and a father? Sears is going to support you. He was here this morning and told me all about it. You might as well say he's adopting you as his son. If you're ever going to be a man, Penn, this isn't the way."

Penn jumped up and stood staring down at him. His eyes looked very dark. "How fit am I? Well, listen to this. Martin Sears isn't supporting me, no matter what he thinks. I never wanted any part of it, and Shelley doesn't either. I've found us a place to live in Limerock, a two-room apartment in the attic of an old lady's house, and we get it rent-free for me doing the work around the place. We've got enough between us to eat on till I'm through school. Then I'm going to work at Atlantic Algin, and I got this job *myself,* Geordie, the same way I got the apartment. And I'll do the rest of it myself too. That's the way we both want it." He stopped, and Geordie could hear his harsh breathing; or was it his own? After a moment Penn said, "Nobody but me is going to pay for our baby. Nobody is going to own him and us but each other."

Geordie stood up too, and the brothers stood close to each other, blue eyes on a level, black heads rigidly high, chins jutting. But inside Geordie was shaken with the explosive knowledge that in the same situation he might have spoken exactly as Penn did. And while Penn was defying him he had felt the spreading warmth of something very like pride.

Everything he'd used to fight with had been the truth. He wouldn't go back on that. But Penn could be speaking the truth too. Only time would tell how right either of them had been.

"If you mean it about the rent in Limerock, and the job," he said slowly, "I'll sign."

"If I mean it!" Penn's eyes were glistening. "I can prove it to you! Come on down and call the old lady up. She's Mrs. Strout on Chestnut Avenue——"

"I dunno about those two rooms. You'll need another one just for your clothes." Geordie began to laugh. It almost hurt, it felt so strange. But it came easier and easier and Penn was laughing too. Neither of them knew why.

Finally Penn blew his nose and said thickly, "I've got to go tell her. Can I take the pickup?"

"Sure, if you don't mind driving up to the Sears' front door in it, and on a Sunday afternoon too."

"Listen, they've got to get used to my Cameron ways and they might as well start now." He reached out suddenly and squeezed Geordie's shoulder, and then whirled around and headed for the stairs.

16

THE WEDDING was to be a simple home ceremony on the next Sunday, when the twins would be back. Mr. Sears was anxious that all the Camerons should be there. Geordie, much to Lucy's surprise, had consented to be Penn's best man. A cousin of Shelley's was to be the one bridesmaid.

Now Lucy told Genie the circumstances, and cautioned her not to be upset if anyone made remarks. "Ignore them. It's nobody's business but Penn's and Shelley's. They made the mistake, and they're the ones who have to work it out." Though it didn't seem as if they were suffering very much these days.

Genie was pale with shock. "I knew they were in love, but gorry, that's no excuse!"

"I hope you'll remember that when you think *you're* in love."

The twins came back, boiling over with the miracles of the week just passed, boiling over again with the excitement of the wedding. And then it was over, the children were back in school, and Penn and Shelley were living in their apartment in Limerock. To Lucy it still seemed unfair that Penn and Shelley could simply seize for themselves what she and Scott wanted so much but had to wait for. And she couldn't understand why Geordie was so mysteriously improved in disposition.

"Aren't you *jealous?*" she blurted out to him the first time they were alone after the wedding. "It looks as if Penn's got everything again—he's being rewarded instead of punished. It's just what you said when you first heard about it."

He looked surprised. "For Pete's sake, you begged me to sign———"

"I'm glad you did. But oh, darn it, Geordie—those two being all snug together under their own roof—I guess I just plain envy them, and I shouldn't."

"You've got a right to," said Geordie, but she didn't find out what he was really thinking.

Maybe, if Geordie had been rigidly truthful with himself, he would have admitted that he'd been jealous of Penn at times. But now, just to be friends with Penn and to feel an honest respect for him was a relief. If only Penn didn't do anything to let him down. . . . He shrugged that off as borrowing trouble, and went out to set more traps for the spring fishing. Would this be the year when he made enough to start paying for a new boat? If he thought hard enough about that, he wouldn't be all fouled up with memories of Donna last spring. A certain picnic out on the Nuggets on an April day; walking on the harbor point in a wild southeast storm, holding hands and dodging the breakers; moonlight and the scent of wild apple blossoms behind the

Grange Hall, and the music from the dance seeming a world away.

He'd had a mother and father then, too. He could hardly recognize now the boy he'd been then. And seeing the geese flying north, and the grass greening on Copper, where they'd picnicked, he knew the boy was not really gone. He felt both excitement and sadness.

Usually Mike Tolman was hauling somewhere else when Geordie was at the Nuggets, as if he were willing to leave Geordie's traps alone but didn't want to catch a glimpse of their owner. But on a blustery Saturday Geordie saw the boat tied up at the wharf, and wondered dryly if it were even leakier than his. Sheets snapped in the wind, and as a heavy cloud came over, darkening the day, the wife came out to collect her washing. She looked all around her as if to search the sea, and when she saw Geordie, she froze. Mischievously he waved, and after a moment she waved back. Instantly Mike appeared at the door of the camp and stared. With a grin Geordie waved at him too, but got nothing more than the hard stare.

Then the rain broke on them, and a squall turned the water feather-white. Geordie had to get out of there quick. Though the rain soon let up, the winds stayed squally the rest of the day, and by the time he'd sold his lobsters, gassed up, and was heading home, he was bone-tired from being on his feet all day in a pitching, rolling boat.

He was depressed too. He'd seen Donna on the wharf. She'd been wearing a pink slicker and sou'wester, and she'd been laughing up at the man beside her, and holding his arm. The laughter had gone when she saw Geordie looking up at her from the boat. Her eyes went wide and she'd said crossly, "I'm about frozen, Jim. Let's get out of this wind." They'd gone.

Freeze, freeze, Geordie snarled in his head. I wish you would, and him with you. . . . He hadn't seen the man's face, only her hand tucked in the crook of the elbow, and he thought he never would forget it. Maybe he *was* jealous of Penn after all, for being sure of Shelley. At least as sure as seventeen-year-olds could be.

He was glad that the twins had slipped up on their duties today and weren't at the wharf to meet him. He stood there a few minutes listening to the seas building up outside the cove, then took his dinnerbox and slogged up the muddy path. Scott's car was in the driveway, nothing unusual on a Saturday. Neither was the noise coming out of the kitchen.

While he was kicking off his boots in the entry Harold heard him and began to bark. "That must be Geordie now!" somebody called. The inside door was opened by one of the twins, and Harold lunged joyously at him. "Hey, Geordie, we got company!" the twin yelled.

His eyebrows drawn against the light, Geordie went into the kitchen. He felt stupid and prematurely old. Scott's brother Craig was there with Linda. He said boisterously, "What do you do, haul 'em by flashlight? We were just about to go looking for you!"

Linda giggled. "What in, the twins' skiff?"

Lucy was pulling at his arm. "Come and wash up,

139

Geordie. Have some coffee and warm apple pie. It'll hold you till supper's ready." She sounded flustered. "They all drove out to have beans with us, and they brought——"

"You arrange this?" he asked from the corner of his mouth.

"No, she didn't," Scott answered under cover of the general conversation. "Blame us. Craig and I got so hungry for the best baked beans in Port George that we came out here and begged at the door."

"The real reason is their folks are visiting upcountry," said Lucy. "They'd have to get their own supper." She looked adoringly at Scott, as Donna had looked up at the faceless man from under the pink sou'wester.

Geordie turned abruptly to the sink and began washing his hands. "I don't want any pie," he said.

"Oh, *Geordie!*" she whispered. "Please be nice for a little while. It's not just Craig and Linda."

He took the towel she pushed at him, wondering in quiet fury why they'd all picked this time to show up, why everything had to be the way it was, why he couldn't walk out of the room without speaking to anyone and go to his room, and stay there until he felt like leaving it again. Next year sometime. . . . Scott he didn't mind, but the rest, and whoever had come with them.

Still without looking at anyone he took his cup and went over to his knitting rocker, set the cup on the windowsill and began to work on a traphead. Craig and Scott were talking, Lucy and Linda fussing around the stove. He became aware of a flurry of whispers apart from the other voices. The twins were urging something, and Genie joined them in it.

"Sing it, sing it," she said. "He'll like it. He loves music."

There was a waiting like a held breath, then the silvery chime of guitar chords, and someone began to sing in a cool, true, unornamented voice, soft in the crowded kitchen, yet sure of itself. All other voices ceased until there was only one.

"When you're done roaming,
  Come home in the gloaming,
  There's aye a warm welcome for you, Geordie mine;
  Cold is the winter blast,
  Stay till the storm is past,
  Peace and rest, home is best, dear Geordie mine."

His own name struck him like an arrow between the shoulders. His thoughts rushed but got nowhere. How could they do this to him? He hated them all. Even Lucy was no longer friend.

"A mavis is a thrush in Scotland," Genie whispered in his ear, and it was like a speech out of a crazy dream. The singing went on, quiet, gentle, sad, like a little wind rising and then falling away to silence.

"Mavis will sing again,
  Curlew will call;
  Heather will bloom again, ere the leaves fall,
  So when you're done roaming
  Come home in the gloaming,
  Home to your bonnie glen, Geordie o' mine."

The room was silent, and then someone sighed. Genie said softly, "Christy, if I could sing like that . . .

141

and play the guitar like that. But it must take years."

He was so hot he was sweating. He turned in his chair and looked across the room and met the gray eyes of the girl on the wharf. She was not smiling as she looked back. What did she *want?* Why had she attacked him with the song? Across the still room he attacked her with a question.

"Any more to it? You'd better get it over with."

She brushed her hand over the strings, then started to speak. But her answer was drowned in a flurry of nervous activity from the other girls, with dishes and silver, and he only got a word or two. He couldn't tell whether she said, "There isn't time," or "This isn't the time."

Her name was Christy Bain, her father was an illustrator, her mother was dead. She was going to college. So far they were renting the house in Port George, but her father had decided to buy it as his Christmas present to her, because she so loved the old house on the harbor shore, with the sound of the sea splashing on the rocks below her window at night.

All this information came from Linda. Christy talked mostly to the younger ones, who were fascinated with her and her guitar. Geordie looked at her now and then, when he thought he wouldn't be noticed, and decided she was as embarrassed as he was. If she'd thought she'd get anywhere, singing a song with his name in it, she knew now it was a brainless mistake.

There was more singing after supper, with everybody but Geordie joining in. Christy wouldn't sing alone, just calmly kept refusing, though she helped carry the rest through the weak places. Geordie supposed he should be pleased that the twins and Genie were having such a good time.

The evening broke up early. Geordie was civil enough to compliment Linda on the cake she'd brought and to say good night to Christy Bain, though he wasn't hearty about it. Neither was she. Grimly he granted her good marks for that.

When the younger ones had gone up to bed, Lucy lit into him. "You were just terrible!"

"What'd I do?"

"It was what you *didn't* do! I don't know what Christy thought!"

"Who cares what Christy thinks?" he growled. "And if I'd felt like putting myself out, my good intentions would have gone up the chimney when she sprang that song on me."

"It wasn't her idea," Lucy retorted. "She sang it earlier, because it's Scotch and we've got Scotch blood, and we all thought it was pretty, and the kids couldn't get over it having your name in it. So they wanted you to hear it. She did it to please them. Halfway through, she was ready to stop, she felt so foolish. You should have seen her blush. You were so darned obvious about just *enduring* it. Only she kept on going, and that took courage."

"Took something," said Geordie dryly.

"I could throw something at you, Geordie Cameron!"

"Anything as long as it's not Christy Bain."

"Why do you hate her?" Lucy was incredulous.

"I don't hate her," said Geordie reasonably. "I just don't give a damn. That clear enough? And I resent you fellers trying to cook up something with me as the soupbone. Now I'm going to bed. Okay?"

"*Okay!*" she snapped. "Nobody's trying to marry you off, for heaven's sake."

"Good night," said Geordie firmly, and went upstairs.

~~~~~~

17

SPRING was on the way, though the way was a long one. Daffodils began to poke up in the lee of the house, and there was a different scent from the ground, even from the ocean. The banking of spruce boughs smelled in the noon warmth like the woods in midsummer heat. The birds were beginning to come back and join those who never left.

Lucy, Ralph, and Genie sat on the front steps in the late afternoon of an April day while the twins took turns riding Ralph's bike in the driveway, paced noisily by Harold. Ralph, that prime source of information, gave Lucy the latest news. Among other items there was one about Christy Bain.

"She's going to give guitar and banjo lessons free this summer to any kids who are really interested."

"I'm interested!" cried Genie, and then slumped. "Heck, I haven't got either a guitar or a banjo."

"Why don't we go over to the dump?" suggested Ralph. "Somebody's down from New York cleaning out the Holliston house, and they're lugging a pile of good stuff to the dump."

"Hey, can we go?" Bike forgotten, the twins gathered round.

"I'll drive you all over after school tomorrow," Lucy promised. She felt relaxed and lazy, and remembered the days she'd come home from school to find her mother out here, trowel or sewing idle near by. It made her lonely, yet it was a comfort too, bringing her mother closer to her.

Suddenly Harold barked, and from the lane came unmistakable sounds. "Somebody's stuck!" yelled Peter. "Come on!" The twins and Harold were off and running, Ralph got in a little track practice behind them, and the two girls followed him.

When they turned into the lane they saw the boys gathered around a new Buick.

"It's Mrs. Morey," whispered Genie in awe.

Lucy hadn't met Ralph's mother face to face since the telephone conversation last fall. But Ralph had been allowed to come back, so there was no need to be nervous now.

"Maybe she's collecting for the Red Cross," she said. "We'll ask her in for a cup of tea." She'd show her best Cameron manners.

Suddenly the twins turned away from the car, looking oddly subdued. Ralph was scarlet; even his ears flamed. Mrs. Morey stood by the car, an angular, handsome woman in tweed skirt and car coat. She said in a much too quiet voice, "I thought I made it clear to you last fall that I didn't want Ralph out here again."

Lucy felt as if she'd been punched in the stomach. But Genie's fingers nervously squeezing her arm were a help. "You did," she said. "But then Ralph came again, and I asked him——" She looked at Ralph, who went even redder. "Mrs. Morey, do you mean that Ralph's been coming here all the time without you knowing it?"

"I do. I found out just today. All this time I thought he was going to another boy's house to study."

"Ralph," said Lucy softly. "I *asked* you——"

"I'm sorry," Ralph mumbled.

"I'm not condoning Ralph's lies," his mother stated. "I'll take that up with him, never fear. And if he should ever show up here again, please do me the kindness of telling him to leave immediately."

"Hey, Mum, don't," Ralph protested feebly. Lucy felt the helpless, humiliated tears clog her throat, she longed for someone to defend her and Genie, but there was no one. The twins' eyes were huge. Genie began to tremble, and it was this that filled Lucy with strong and reviving rage.

"Mrs. Morey," she said softly, "what's wrong with us? Do you think Ralph's learning anything bad out here? Don't worry, I won't let him come if you don't want him to, but would you please tell me *why?*"

Mrs. Morey's eyes flickered behind her glasses. She said, "I don't have to explain myself to you. You're only a child yourself. Ralph, get into the car."

"We aren't going anywhere right off, Mum," he said with something like relish. "You've ground her right to the hubcaps in front."

"Will you please tell me, Mrs. Morey?" Lucy persisted.

"We aren't *going* together!" Genie blurted. "We're just friends!"

"I'm not attacking your character," Mrs. Morey said from stiff lips. "It's just the whole picture. You run wild out here. Not bad, but wild. There's no adult supervision. . . . Ralph never lied to me in his life till he started spending all his free time out here. And he'd never have become a liar if he hadn't been under the influence of this place."

"None of us are liars, Mrs. Morey," Lucy said. She felt just fine, she was so mad.

"I didn't say you were. But this is the way I happen to feel about Ralph. When he's through college and self-supporting, then he can do as he pleases."

I'll bet, Lucy thought. Not if he still lives in Port George.

"Until then," said Mrs. Morey with icy precision, "his duty is to us, and he can't do it when he's running wild. He's our only son, and that places a great responsibility on his shoulders as well as ours."

"I asked you not to say stuff to them, Mum," Ralph said warningly. "I asked you not to, but you did, so I'm asking *you* something. Why didn't you have brothers and sisters for me so I'd have the fun at home I have out here? No, all you and Dad could think about was the store. I suppose you couldn't take the time to think about any more kids! It's a wonder you even had *me!*"

Mrs. Morey had gone a queer grayish white. She looked at Ralph as if she'd never seen him before, and Lucy wanted to tell him to stop, but she couldn't. It was as if every word were striking his mother like a fist.

"You know what that house is like?" he asked. "To come home to and sit down to do my homework in? Almost every day since I was a little kid, and evenings too, a lot of the time? It's some old, empty, without even a cat or a dog in it." He gathered new fire. "Yeah, why couldn't I have a dog of my own?"

"You were allergic——"

"Harold doesn't make me sneeze!" He grabbed Harold and shoved his face into the dog's neck, breathed deeply, then grinned at his mother. "See?"

She put her hand on the car door. "Ralph," she said coldly. "I'll start walking to town and send someone out to get the car. You get your bicycle and come along." Only Lucy saw how she gripped the door handle, as if to hold her up.

"I can call the garage," she said. "You could wait in the car."

Without answering, Mrs. Morey got into the car and sat down. "I better get my bike," Ralph muttered, looking nervous and worried. Genie didn't offer to walk back to the house with him and he went alone, the rest trailing behind him.

Silently he took his bicycle and went back to the lane. Watching him go, Genie said bitterly, "He could have said something. He never even looked at us."

"What could he say?" asked Lucy. "He probably never spoke to his mother like that before, and he's all upset. The way she looked upset *me*." She called the garage, forbade the twins to go back to the lane to see the car hauled out, and sent them to the shore to gather driftwood and pile it out of the tide's way. "In case we want

149

a picnic one of these days," she told them. They rushed off with Harold. Then she turned to Genie.

"It was all just words," she said. "She's only got Ralph, and it's a wonder she hasn't protected him to death. She looked terrible when he asked her why she didn't have any others. Maybe she wanted them, but couldn't have them. Maybe some died, that Ralph doesn't know about. Anyway, I felt sorry for her, and I'm plenty sorry for Ralph."

"It doesn't matter why she said it," Genie said. "She said it. He can't come here anymore. And what are we going to *do?*" Tears were in her voice. "We're each other's best friends. We know each other's thoughts before we say them, we're like two halves of one person. I mean we *were*. But she's ruined it, Luce." The tears ran down her face.

Lucy put her arms around her. "She can't spoil what you've had, honey." But she knew that was no answer for Genie. "Think of what poor Ralph's going through right now," she said, but Genie pulled away from her and ran outdoors, toward the woods.

18

G EORDIE heard about it before he reached the house, courtesy of the twins. When he came in he was wearing his most granite face. Genie had returned, and was being very quiet as she set the table.

"Listen," Geordie said to her. "You're not to speak to him, again, you understand? You don't even see him. He doesn't exist."

Genie's eyes grew big and black. Suddenly she threw the silver halfway across the room, and in the crash of cutlery and Harold's alarmed barking she ran out of the room and upstairs.

"Jeepers!" Peter breathed.

"Boys, pick it up for me, please," Lucy said, "and then go into the sitting room and study your spelling words."

"Can't we watch tel——"

"No," said Geordie, and they left rapidly. He dropped into the captain's chair and ran his hands over his face.

"I don't know what the twins told you, but I can imagine it didn't lose anything," said Lucy. "There's no need of being that stiff with Genie." He waited, one eyebrow lifted in a way that always annoyed her. She told him what happened.

"That doesn't change anything," he said curtly. "We're an evil influence out here, so Genie doesn't corrupt the white hen's chick any more by speaking to him. For two cents I'd drop into the store and tell Morey so."

"Geordie Cameron, don't you dare!"

"All right. But don't *you* go underrunning me. This was coming sooner or later, and now we can get it over with."

Lucy shrugged and began putting the newly washed silver around. "How are the lobsters coming?"

"Fair. They're beginning to crawl in from deep water now."

"Any trouble with Mike Tolman?"

"Nope. He's a cat in a strange garret, and knows it. I saw him off Sea Horse Ledge today. Had his wife and kids with him."

"I wonder if she's lonely out on Gold, or if she loves it so much she doesn't care if she ever comes ashore." Geordie didn't answer. She thought enviously that Mike Tolman's wife was with her husband in a little world all their own, and forced her mind back to the day's events.

"Do you suppose Mrs. Morey's busy telling everybody that the kids ought to be taken away from us?"

Geordie roused himself from morose speculation. "It takes more than talk. Everybody knows the way they are about Ralph. But——" He sighed heavily. "Times like this, you wonder just how capable you are, and it looks like a heck of a long road ahead. Penn's given us one surprise, and we don't know what Genie's likely to get into, if she's hurt bad enough."

"Genie's sensible!" Lucy flared. "And she's pure and idealistic!"

"And she's good-looking, and growing up, and ready to fall in love. And after she's grown, we've got the twins coming along. I wonder what they've got in store for us. I wonder if we can handle it, whatever it is."

"Geordie," she said in a low voice, "are you by any chance saying we should let them go?"

They looked into each other's faces for a long moment. Then, just as he opened his mouth, she thought she heard someone on the stairs, and she opened the kitchen door and went into the hall. The living room door was ajar, and she could see Peter curled up in a big chair, writing out his words. So Philip must be there too.

Genie wouldn't come down for supper and she didn't want anything to eat. It was an uncomfortable meal. Lucy and Geordie tried to make conversation, about safe subjects, but the twins ate in unusual silence, apparently still upset by the afternoon's scene or hatching up something as they felt the stir of spring.

"Peter and Pip, didn't you do something up in Boston that you haven't told us about yet?" Lucy asked.

Philip shrugged and kept on eating. Peter frowned as if trying to think, then said, "Nope." After that Lucy gave up. She was very tired all at once; as Geordie had said, it looked like a heck of a long road ahead.

They all went to bed early, and she took up a small thermos bottle of cocoa and some wrapped bread and butter in case Genie felt like eating later. She was huddled under her bedclothes and mumbled, "Thanks." The very tone warned Lucy to stay away.

Genie got up at her usual time. She seemed more preoccupied with a math quiz than anything else. "Thanks for the mug-up," she said. "I woke up around four o'clock and had it then, while I was studying for my test."

"Well, I hope you can stay awake for it," Lucy said, which got a faint smile from Genie. The twins came downstairs with chips on their shoulders, and the first blow was struck before they got to the table. It took Lucy and Genie both to separate them, while Harold decided to see what was on someone's plate.

There was a thick fog that morning, so Geordie hadn't gone out but was busy in the fishhouse. When they'd all left for school, Geordie came up to the house.

"Coward," said Lucy.

"Why?"

"The twins were just awful."

"Oh, it's spring fever, the weather, growing pains." He broke eggs into the frying pan. "Want some?"

"No, thanks. . . . How come you're so philosophic this morning? Last night you talked as if you'd had it."

He grinned at her. "My trouble's the same as theirs. Spring fever, the weather, growing pains. I'll get 'em down to the fishhouse after school and they can start painting the skiff. That'll cheer 'em up."

"Last night you didn't think you could manage them."

"Ayuh, but this morning I could lick my weight in small boys any time. . . . How was Genie?"

"Pretty good. But I don't know how she'll feel when she sees him on the bus," she said worriedly. "He still exists even if you told her he doesn't."

"Don't fuss." He filled his plate. "She'll survive. If this is the worst thing that ever happens to her she'll be lucky."

His mood was contagious and by the time the sun burned through the fog and the wind came roistering around to the northwest, she was cheerfully cleaning Penn's room. The twins could now have separate quarters.

When the children came home Geordie was at the house. "I want you men down at the fishhouse, dressed for painting, in twenty minutes," he told the twins. "No lallygagging now."

"Why should we paint the skiff?" Peter defied him.

"She's yours, isn't she? You don't think I'm going to fix her up, do you?"

"After we get her all fixed up," Philip said tightly, "you'll likely sell her." Then he walked stiffly out of the room, Peter after him.

"I heard on the bus that Pip got sent to Mr. Gordon's office," Genie said. Then she gave them a funny, twisted little smile. "You don't have to worry about me speaking to Ralph. He wasn't on the bus."

"They driving him back and forth to save him from corruption?" asked Geordie.

"They've sent him to stay with his grandmother in

Limerock. He comes to school on his bike . . . and he kind of slides around me. I guess he's had his orders too." She walked straight out of the house and they watched her go toward the path that led up the rise. The snow was all gone now and the song sparrows sang from the bare alders. The brown slopes looked gold in the afternoon sun, fair-weather clouds rushed across a blue sky, and there was a warm edge to the boisterous wind.

"She'll be as well off outdoors today as anywhere," Lucy said sadly.

"I guess I will tell Morey something," said Geordie.

"No, you won't. You'll straighten out those twins."

Geordie rubbed his long jaw hard, shook his head, and went down to the fishhouse.

~~~~~~

19

O N HER fifteenth birthday Genie declared a kind of independence. She printed a neat "Job Wanted" notice and posted it on the bulletin board in the store. She would do baby-sitting, and help with spring housecleaning or general housework. Lucy and Geordie approved, hoping that the new projects would do something for her. She had been much too quiet in the last month, spending too much time alone, losing interest in school activities, though she worked hard at her lessons.

The twins finally got the skiff painted, though Geordie had to drive them to it, and now she was anchored in the cove, soaking up. He'd expected that they'd keep pestering to row, but they showed a disappointing lack of interest. All their interest seemed to be centered on trouble.

They threw their clothes around, broke so many dishes when they wiped them that Lucy gave up on that. They were defiant or impudent, they ran off into the woods or around the shore without notice, and stayed out long past the supper hour, while the older ones called and called.

Geordie tried several approaches short of spankings, but nothing worked for long. They watched him with big eyes that told him nothing, and he felt he was getting exactly nowhere. At last he received a call from the principal at school, and he came back angry and perplexed.

"I'll be darned if it's all spring fever," he told Lucy that night. "It's downright deviltry." The twins had been sent to bed right after supper, television suspended for a week. "Mr. Gordon can't understand it either."

Lucy thought, How can I ever leave Genie in charge here? She couldn't possibly manage those boys. Even if I'm only a few miles away, I'd be no good to her that way. . . . She wanted to cry. Everything was so *unfair*.

"I've been itching to wallop them," Geordie was saying. "But then I take hold of one and he feels about as big as a kitten to me." He held up one hand and scowled at it. "I think one swipe with this and I could break a bone."

"You always said they never got enough spankings."

"Well, I'm beginning to see Pa's viewpoint," he said dourly. The front legs of his chair came down with a bang. "Luce, let's leave ourselves and our feelings out of it. Say we're no relation to the kids and we're looking on from the outside. We thought the kids would never want to leave us, but maybe we're wrong. Do you realize all this deviltry started *after* they'd been to Boston?"

She grabbed at a straw. "Not *right* after!"

"Soon enough so I'm getting the notion that they want to go away, and I don't know as I blame 'em. Like Penn said, they'll have everything. And we could stop worrying about them and think about ourselves for a change."

"Is that what you want, Geordie?" It was hard to ask. But his face was answer enough as he shook his head.

There was a thump upstairs and Lucy looked up at the ceiling. "Harold's scratching. I'll have to get after him with flea powder tomorrow. . . . I hope *he* doesn't start acting up, chasing deer or cars or something."

"Thank God he's past his adolescence," said Geordie.

Genie got a baby-sitting job at once with a friend of Scott's married sister; she got off the school bus in the village in the afternoons and went right to the Merrill house to take care of the eighteen-month-old boy until six, when Mr. Merrill drove her home.

She was almost naturally cheerful at the end of the first day. "Davy's a doll, and he just loves to ride in his carriage, so we walked all over the village. He gets so excited about everything!" She looked around. "Where are the kids, down baiting up?"

"That'll be the day," said Lucy. "They used to be crazy about it. Now they'd run a mile from it. The last time, they got into a fight and plastered the fishhouse and each other with salt herring, remember? Well, Geordie can't afford to waste good bait like that."

"He ought to give them a good spanking."

"He doesn't think that'd solve anything. Genie, have you heard them say anything about being with the Sylvesters?"

Genie looked blank. "They talk about it now and

then, something they saw, where they went, what the kids do up there. . . . And they think Boston's like Wonderland, of course."

"Mmm. . . . Well, go out and give a shout, will you? They've disappeared again."

At the end of three weeks Genie bought a guitar from a girl at school. "I don't care about a bike now," she said somberly. "But playing a guitar and singing is something you can do by yourself." Her loneliness wrung Lucy's heart.

But a few days later, when she came home from her job, her eyes looked happier than they'd been for weeks. "Can you spare me for all day tomorrow? And drive me in real early? I'm going to make ten dollars out of it!"

"Cleaning?" Lucy asked.

"Nope! They're going to Portland for the day, and it's the first time they ever left Davy that long before. They really trust me." She looked soberly pleased. "I plan to take him on a good long walk all around town in the afternoon. He loves that."

"That'll be nice," Lucy said cautiously, never knowing how Genie was going to take things these days. Ralph came home on weekends and worked in the drugstore. She wondered if Lucy were prepared for seeing him tomorrow, or if she'd be careful not to wheel the stroller past the store.

~~~~~~

20

W ITH THE twins and Harold in the back of the truck, Lucy drove Genie into town the next morning, so the Merrills could leave at nine. Geordie had gone out to haul by six. After dropping Genie and admiring young Davy, Lucy stopped at the store for a grocery order and also at the post office. Here she asked the three in back who wanted to come in front with her.

"Nobody!" the twins shouted, but Harold always responded to the word "want," so he was transferred to the front seat. Lucy sang as she drove home, with Harold helping on the high notes. The day was full of just-arrived birds, and scented with new grass and the sea. Out there on the shimmering blue bay Geordie was catching a lot of lobsters. Penn and Shelley were all right for now, Genie was on her way to being all right, and Lucy found it hard to believe the twins would be difficult on such a day.

They can't want to leave us! she thought. Just a week away couldn't change them. They'd been too happy to get home. . . . I'm going to ask them straight out, Lucy decided. Oh, we keep saying, *Why did you do this or that,* but we always say that anyway, and they look stupid, and say, *I dunno,* or *I wanted to,* or *He made me,* or *I didn't.*

But if I kept after them, *really* kept after them . . . I'll soften them up first with a picnic out on the end of the point.

"Now, kids," she said, heading into the kitchen, "you make your beds and tidy your rooms, and I'll see what we've got for lunch, and we'll take off for the point. Nobody's beachcombed around there for a long time and there ought to be a lot of good stuff." She began opening cupboard doors and looking things over. But there was silence, where there should have been applause. She turned. There was only Harold, hopefully watching her. She heard the boys upstairs.

She decided on corned-beef-and-pickle sandwiches, and went down cellar to get a can of the meat. While she was there she picked out some of her own blackberry jam to go with hot biscuits tonight. Harold, who loved to go down cellar, snuffled suspiciously in corners. Suddenly he looked up, listened, and then rushed for the stairs. She heard him running overhead, and smiled. He was forever checking on the children.

When she came upstairs she knew the house was empty of dog and children, but they'd be either out around the barn or down on the beach. She made up the sandwiches and a jug of fruit punch, added bananas and cookies to the basket, and was ready.

But the children weren't. They were nowhere. She called, she whistled for Harold, who didn't come. She went out to the barn, where only the newly arrived barn swallows darted back and forth. She checked the beach and the fishhouse. She went to see if they were looking for early violets in the old pasture. But everywhere only birds greeted her.

She went back to the house and searched the rooms upstairs and the attic, to see if it was all a big joke on her. Still, how could they keep Harold so quiet?

Then, with relief, she decided they must have already started off to the point. She took the basket and the jug and set off, confident that they'd be climbing around the big tawny rocks when she got there.

The lack of them here knocked the breath out of her. She sat down abruptly on a rock. Her legs felt trembly. If this was a joke, it was a rotten one, and she'd let them know it. There'd be no picnic unless they apologized.

"They certainly do need spankings," she said aloud, to cover the fact that she was not so much angry as frightened.

But why should she be afraid? They'd probably gone up into the woods behind the house to hide, holding onto Harold so he couldn't come when she whistled. She had a good mind to stay out here for a while, so that when they got tired of their joke they'd return to an empty house and could wonder about *her* for a while.

But she couldn't relax, and finally started back. The house still had its deserted look, and an hour later the silence was beginning to throb in Lucy's ears. There was plenty she could do around the place, but she couldn't settle down to it.

Anyway, she scolded herself, they'll be back when they're hungry. This is life, not science-fiction. They haven't been stolen by a flying saucer.

163

Noontime came, and the prevailing southwest wind began to spring up, turning the bay blue-green and choppy. She walked on the shore again, calling and whistling till her mouth was too dry. Then she thought they might have gone up to the main road and started walking. They'd been talking about some fossil rocks a boy had found at a beach which the black road passed.

She ran to the truck.

There were fossil hunters at the beach, but not hers. She drove into town and asked at the store and around the wharves, but no one had seen them. She went to the Merrills', convinced they must have gone there. But Genie, just getting Davy ready for his nap, hadn't seen them. Lucy called several boys' homes, with no results. She was ready to explode with panic now, but she couldn't give in when Genie was so frightened.

"You settle Davy in his crib," she said briskly, "and I'll think what to do next. Don't act nervous, because it will upset him." As Genie went upstairs, making an effort to talk nonsense to the baby, Lucy longed for Scott. But before she called him she'd see if the twins had gone home.

No one answered at the house, and there was something devasting about the ring going on and on. She hung up, to face Genie's pallor and trembling lips. She said in comfort, "They'd be outside somewhere, anyway."

"Shouldn't we—shouldn't we call the Coast Guard—" Genie swallowed—"and they can find Geordie and send him home?" She looked sick; they'd called the Coast Guard the night their father hadn't come home.

"I'll call Scott," Lucy decided, "and ask him."

At the sound of his voice she almost dissolved. If anything ever happened to him, how could she survive?

"They're probably exploring somewhere, and they've lost track of the time," he said confidently. "I've done the same thing when I was their age. Look, honey, you go on home, and if they aren't around the place, call me back. Okay?"

"Okay." She turned eagerly to go, and met Genie's terror. Lucy hugged her. "Look, you have to stay here, that's your job. But I'll call you as soon as I can." She couldn't help thinking what a help Ralph would have been right now. "Don't panic, sweetie, think of Davy and that ten dollars. The twins are likely eating my picnic lunch right now." They both tried to laugh, and she hurried out.

But at Cameron Cove only the increasing wind met her, with a salty slap in the face. As she stood there trying to get up the strength to go in and call Scott, she saw *Mary C.* coming up the cove. It was far too early for Geordie to be coming in, and she thought at first that Genie had panicked and called the Coast Guard anyway. But the boat was coming very slowly, a sign of trouble with engine or propeller. She ran out on the wharf as Geordie brought the boat alongside.

He scowled up at her. "Where's the kids' skiff?"

"I didn't even notice she was missing!" Lucy gasped.

"What's happened?" He came fast up the ladder.

She told him. When he realized how long they'd been gone, a groan almost came from him, but he kept it back. Lucy looked about ready to fall apart, and he couldn't give in to the fear that was trying to liquefy his own bones.

"Well, they didn't head to the north," he said, "because I've been hauling up that way all day, and that fresh white paint would show up against the shore. I'll call Sam Cady, and if anybody's come in, he can send 'em out again. If nobody's in yet we'll get the Coast Guard." He squeezed her arm. "Don't worry, Luce."

"I'm t-trying not to. . . . Call Scott instead of Sam. He's waiting, and he can see from the office if there's anybody in."

There was nobody in, but Craig hadn't gone out today because he was sick. Scott would take Craig's boat and follow from the harbor toward Cameron Cove, contacting other fishermen by radio telephone as he went along.

"Thanks, Scott," Geordie said evenly. "I've got a warp in my wheel so I can just jog, but I'm going out anyway." He hung up. Lucy was pulling on a jacket.

"I'm going with you," she said.

"Bring the glasses." He went on out. Lucy didn't follow directly, and when in a few minutes she swung down the ladder into the boat he said ferociously, "What kept you?"

"I promised to call Genie, but instead I called the Howells and asked the girls to go and stay with her."

"*Good.*" He chopped off the word.

The slowness of the boat drove him into a fury. His hand kept shaking on the wheel, and he kept the other deep in his pocket. When he wasn't seeing the overturned skiff splintering in the breakers he was remembering the day his father had drowned. He didn't dare imagine the children's faces, or even Harold.

Lucy watched the shore with binoculars while Geordie tried to keep the slowly moving boat jogging up into the wind, so the roughening seas wouldn't push her toward the land. The hard spanking and jouncing was bad for her, but he couldn't think of that now.

Once Lucy cried out, and then said, "No, I guess it's an old crate."

The seas were deepening and the bow came down hard, and spray flew back over them. Enough of this, and the boat would start leaking badly. Down to the southward Geordie saw Craig's *Duchess*. Another boat appeared from behind a high ledge and veered toward her. This was how they'd begun gathering to search for his father. He felt sick enough to vomit.

Another boat was coming from the Nuggets, running ahead of following seas toward *Mary C*. As she grew larger and clearer, he recognized Mike Tolman's boat. He had no radio, so he wouldn't know about the search. His head poked out past the sprayhood, and he waved one arm wildly.

If he's missing a couple of traps and blames me, Geordie thought, I'm going to let him have it right in the mouth.

Mike waved even more wildly. As the angle of approach changed slightly, Geordie saw a white skiff in tow, riding high. Lucy squeezed his arm with both hands, and he knew she'd seen the skiff too. Numbly he turned the boat toward Mike.

They're dead, he thought. Mike found the skiff drifting. They're dead.

Mike surged up to him, engine throttled down and the
seas carrying the boat along. One moment her bow rose
high above *Mary C.*, then she was down again, and Mike
was leaning past the sprayhood, his grin wide in his thin
sunburnt face.

Three heads rose cautiously above the washboard and
stared across green and white water at Geordie. Two
were red, and the third had prick ears and a joyous bark,
and Mike's wife appeared and grabbed the owner by his
collar before he could jump overboard.

"Can't shift 'em here!" Mike shouted. "I'll take 'em
right to your wharf!"

"All right!" Geordie yelled. The other boat swung a-
way from them. The seas carried *Mary C.* back a lot
faster than she'd come out. Geordie and Lucy didn't
speak. The horror was still too close, they could hardly
believe they'd escaped it.

Duchess was gaining on them and soon was rolling
along abreast, slowed down to keep them company.
Scott was all smiles at the wheel. He had binoculars
around his neck and had evidently seen Mike's passen-
gers. Someone bundled in orange raingear stood beside
him, also carrying field glasses. Not big enough for
Craig, but there was always someone standing around
the shore ready to go along.

Geordie signaled with a sweep of his arm for Scott to
follow into the cove. The Tolman boat was already at
the wharf, and Harold was driving gulls off the posts as if

he hadn't been anywhere. The twins were not to be seen.

"Oh, they high-tailed it up to the house with all their gear," Mike said. "Going to make out it never happened, most likely." His two very little boys sat on the engine box, staring with fascination at Harold's antics.

Mike's wife wasn't the scared kid Geordie had seen before. Laughing, she said, "You'd never believe what they had to camp out with! Salt fish and apples and dog biscuits! They said they were going to live off clams and shore greens."

Mike had discovered them on the seaward side of the small grassy Nugget called Copper when he heard a dog barking and went to investigate. Harold was chasing sea gulls. The twins were making a tent with blankets. They had rowed out on the morning's flat calm sea.

"They didn't take kindly to my interference," said Mike. "Feisty little fellers. Dog was real friendly, though."

"Come on up to the house, please," Lucy begged. "I'll make coffee. We need something."

"Those kids sure need something," said Geordie, "and they're going to get it."

"I guess we better go home," said Mike. Geordie had the grace to blush.

"Oh, come on up," he said. "We're still winded with this, but we'll get over it. We owe you plenty of thanks."

"The look on your faces was thanks enough," said Weezie. "It'll set us up for a year."

Duchess came purring alongside, and then Lucy and

Scott saw only each other. Geordie had to grin. In fact, he kept feeling this silly weak tendency to grin, as if he were drunk. Not that he'd ever been drunk, but this must be something like it. "Meet Scott Barstow, Mike and Weezie Tolman," he said expansively.

"And Allan and Kent Tolman," said Weezie, pointing to her boys. Mike and Scott shook hands across gunnels. Scott's passenger pushed back the parka's hood, and a gust of wind whipped her black hair around her face. She stared straight at Geordie as if to say, "Here I am. What are you going to do about it?"

"Oh, Mike and Weezie," Lucy cried, "this is Christy Bain. She's new here too."

Christy was pleasant and friendly with the Tolmans, she called each little boy by name, but her eyes kept coming back to Geordie. Not timidly or slyly, but as if she wanted to *know* something. He didn't know it was the way he too looked at people, either embarrassing or intriguing them. With this funny feeling he had right now, he didn't mind Christy too much; at least she'd been helping in the search.

"I'm trying to get everybody up to the house for a mug-up," Lucy said to Christy.

"Well, while it's being talked over I'll go up and talk over something with the twins," said Geordie. He walked across the stern deck of Mike's boat to the ladder.

"Geordie, go easy," Lucy called after him. Then, in astonishment, "Look!"

Harold shot off to greet the newcomers. Penn and Shelley were coming down the wharf, and behind them came Genie, and Ralph carrying young Davy. Genie flung herself at Geordie with a frantic hug, and then at Lucy.

"I called Penn, and they came down and got me, and Ralph, and we came right out, and there they were, running for the house like mad! Oh, I never was so happy in all my life!"

Penn was grinning the way Geordie wanted to. Shelley was wiping her eyes and blowing her nose. Ralph sternly clutched the baby, who was shouting "Gog! Gog!" at Harold.

"*Ralph,*" said Lucy softly. "Does your———"

Ralph looked her in the eye. He seemed to have grown much older in the few weeks since she had last seen him. "I don't know," he said. "And I don't care."

"I'll call her myself," she warned him, and he shrugged as much as he could with a heavy baby leaning dangerously out of his arms to wave at Harold, who was strenuously responding.

Geordie left them all behind.

21

B ECAUSE you're going to give us away," Peter said. "That's why. We thought we'd go live on an island and be hermits."

"Where in time did you get that idea?" demanded Geordie. He sat in the captain's chair. The twins stood stiffly before him.

"We *heard* you," Philip accused him. "Twice! And Lucy said something too! We heard you guys talking about it, the day Ralph's mother came."

"We heard you again too," said Peter. "You thought we were asleep."

Geordie said sternly, "So that's why you've been raising the devil around here."

"We got mad at you," said Peter bravely, "because we thought you didn't like us anymore. You said the skiff was ours, but we didn't believe that. We——" He began to sniffle, and rubbed his eyes.

"What was the matter with asking me straight out?"

"We were scared to," Philip said. "We thought you wouldn't tell us."

"That I'd lie, in other words. Have you ever caught me in a lie?" When they shook their heads, and Philip's lip began to tremble, he went on, "I've never lied to you and I don't intend to begin now. The trouble with listening to other people's private conversations is that you only hear about half. We talked about it, sure. The way you were acting around here, we thought you *wanted* to go. But we didn't like thinking it."

"Why didn't you ask *us?*" said Peter in a shaky little voice.

"I should have," Geordie said. Both twins flung themselves on him and wrapped their arms around him. He hugged them very close so they couldn't see his face.

After a few minutes he sent them to wash their faces, and he blew his nose. *"Now,"* he said severely, when they came back from the bathroom. "It's been stated pretty often around here that what you two need is a good hiding. I'm warning you now that if you don't start acting like responsible Camerons, you're going to feel this." He lifted his hand. "Right on the seat of the pants. Is that clear?"

"Yessir!"

"Another thing. In the future I'll ask you what I want to know, and you're to ask me. Is that understood?"

"Yessir!"

"All right. Let's put the teakettle on for a mug-up."

"No, first you have to say it!" cried Philip.

"Say what?" He looked down at them in honest bewilderment, and then he remembered. Squaring his shoulders, putting back his head, he took in a deep breath and shouted, "Come a-board and bring your do-o-ory!"

Outside there was a burst of cheering, handclapping, laughing, and barking. Everyone came streaming in.

173

Penn had the baby on his shoulder. The little Tolmans were entranced with everything, and their mother almost illuminated the place with her pleasure at being there.

"Come in, come in!" Geordie welcomed them all as his father had always welcomed callers. Christy came gravely at the end, and they nodded at one another.

"Oh, Christy," Genie called, "I've got my guitar, so will you tune it for me, and everything?" She ran up to her room.

"Shelley and Ralph, will you get out cups and stuff?" Lucy asked them. She murmured to Geordie, "I've got to call Mrs. Morey. I'll take the telephone around the corner into the bathroom."

"Don't let her throw you."

"Nothing could throw me today." She was almost beautiful in her happiness. Geordie saw Scott watching her as if he'd never seen her before, and he felt a stab of loneliness, not so much for Donna as for what had gone out of his life with her.

Lucy was also feeling a stab, of apprehension, as she dialed the drugstore number. Mrs. Morey answered. Lucy said politely, "Mrs. Morey, Ralph is here. I'll tell him to leave."

"Don't tell him, Lucy." Mrs. Morey's voice was almost too soft to hear. "I knew where he'd gone. When the news reached the store about the twins, Ralph simply walked out without a word to either of us, and we knew he'd gone to Genie. . . . We didn't try to call him back." She stopped, then went on. "Friendship is— friendship. If he's always this loyal to his principles I guess we don't have to worry too much. . . . I haven't quite got over that day yet, to tell you the truth. His father and I—well, we've had to do a little hard thinking. Anyway, you tell him he can have the afternoon off if he'll make it up some other time."

"Thank you very much, Mrs. Morey."

"Lucy, what about the twins?"

Lucy couldn't hold back her joy. "They'd rowed out to the Nuggets! The man out there found them and brought them in!"

"I'm glad. Good-bye, Lucy." She hung up. Feeling rather dazed, Lucy went out to the kitchen and passed the message on to Ralph, then began getting food out.

Geordie stood with one foot on the stove hearth and looked at his busy kitchen. The twins had brought down trucks and boats to entertain the baby and the small boys. Scott and Mike were talking. Penn and Ralph were having an earnest discussion.

"I may go to college yet," Penn was saying. "After I've worked a year. Shelley says we can do it."

The girls' conversation rippled around the rest. Christy wasn't taking any part in it, however. She sat on the tall stool by the telephone, her head bent over the guitar as she tuned it. Genie watched eagerly, cocking her head like Harold to every sound from the strings.

Finally Christy ran her fingers over them in a perfect chord. She smiled at Genie. "It has a lovely tone. You have a nice guitar."

Genie beamed. "Now play us something."

"Genie!" Lucy called. "Will you go down cellar and find some of that grape jelly?"

Genie looked resigned. "Grab a flashlight off the mantel, Ralph, and come on. It's darker than the inside of a cow."

175

"How do you know?" Ralph followed her. "Were you ever inside a cow?"

Christy and Geordie looked at each other and smiled. It was accomplished as swiftly as that. And for the life of him Geordie couldn't remember now why he had ever been hostile to her, unless it was because he'd felt so savage about something else each time, and Christy had got into the line of fire.

They were curiously isolated in their corner of the kitchen. "Is it time now?" Geordie heard himself ask.

She knew what he meant. Leaning her head over the guitar she sang the rest of the song so softly that he thought no one else heard it but him.

> "Haste you back, Geordie mine Over the sea:
>   Soon will our arms entwine, Happy we'll be:
>   So now you're done roaming,
>   Come home in the gloaming,
>   Home to your bonny glen,
>   Geordie o' mine."

Lucy, caught in a little eddy of silence by the stove, heard it and looked at the two with radiant hope. Scott said behind her, "Don't go counting your chickens."

"I'm not. But after Donna I didn't think he'd ever look that way at a girl again. So I can't help being glad." She swung around quickly to search his face, one hand on his shoulder. "You haven't heard anything yet?"

Smiling, he shook his head, and she sighed with satisfaction. "Then we're all right for the weekend, aren't we?"

"We're always all right, Lucy," Scott said.

176